To stop a stage single-handed was pure cussed fool-ishness, but Slocum was too mad to care.

"You inside," Slocum yelled, "come on out here one at a time. The first gun I see means someone dies." They started filing out, two of them looking nervous and two of them looking almost bored.

"I want everyone," Slocum growled. "Where's the woman?"

"There was no woman," said the driver.

"Don't give me that. I was told there was."

"Look for yourself, mister."

The girl had pulled a fast one...

OTHER BOOKS BY JAKE LOGAN

JAKE LOGAN

SLOCUM IN DEADWOOD

BERKLEY BOOKS, NEW YORK

SLOCUM IN DEADWOOD

A Berkley Book/published by arrangement with
the author

PRINTING HISTORY
Berkley edition/September 1984

ISBN: 0-425-07493-5

A BERKLEY BOOK® TM 757,375
Berkley Books are published by The Berkley Publishing Group,
200 Madison Avenue, New York, N.Y. 10016.
The name "BERKLEY" and the stylized "B" with design are trademarks
belonging to Berkley Publishing Corporation.
PRINTED IN THE UNITED STATES OF AMERICA

1

Slocum was attracted by the crowd first, even before he heard the pitchman's loud voice coming from its center.

"Two bits a bar, gents. The lye will keep you clean, and you may find something green. Just twenty-five cents for your lucky bar of soap."

A crowd was something you'd expect to see on a Deadwood street during a spring evening in '77. The fortune hunters and the ones who came to take their fortunes away were still pouring into the Black Hills from every point, and only a few of them ever found a job or a claim to work. The rest of them flowed restlessly through the boom-town streets, men of every stripe who jammed the boardwalks at any hour of the day or night.

"Now I know you gents can use a bar of soap," said the same voice from within the crowd. "Heaven help me, I'm afraid to take a deep breath!"

There was a bit of laughter in the crowd and Slocum smiled, slowing to take a look. It wasn't the crowd that intrigued him at all, but the fact that someone was trying to sell soap in the middle of a gold camp. A bottle of whiskey he could understand, or the ever-popular shell game. But bars of soap? At two bits a crack? They'd have to be as big as a side of beef to be worth that much. Slocum began working his way toward the pitchman, who was just warming up.

"Now look, my friends, this is good lye soap. It's fresh from Cheyenne, and I guarantee it. Hear me? It *will* do the job. It also might change your luck, my friends, because some of these bars are double-wrapped."

Slocum could see the pitchman. He was short and hatless

with unkempt hair and a day's growth of beard on his face, wearing a vest over a wrinkled red shirt. He stood at the tailgate of a freight wagon, beside a mound of perhaps three hundred bars of soap, each wrapped in brown paper.

"Now I'm not saying they're wrapped in two layers of paper," said the pitchman. "Not at all. I'm talking about a genuine gold certificate, a crisp bill worth five dollars!" He pointed at one of the bars in the pile. "Is it this one? I'm afraid I couldn't tell you, because I don't remember. But five of you here tonight will walk away with enough money to live high off the hog for three nights!" The pitchman seemed to have a second thought about prices in a gold camp, and smiled at the crowd with watery eyes. "Well, maybe three hours here in Deadwood."

There were more laughs from the crowd, but no takers. Slocum was now in the second row, directly behind a dandy of some sort who wore a pearl gray suit and carried a thin black cane.

"I can't credit my eyes," yelled the pitchman. "You men are the most adverturesome lot in America! You've gambled hundreds of dollars and even your lives to come and strike it rich. Yet you balk at a quarter of a dollar that could give you a return of twentyfold!"

"Aye, but look at the odds," said someone in the crowd. "I'd say prett' near three hundred of us will be taking very expensive baths."

The men laughed hard at that one, and so did the pitchman, who said, "Yes, but at least you'll be clean, which is more than I can say for you now. And you men all *came* to this dreary gulch precisely because you are gamblers."

The men looked at each other, and finally one of them stepped forward. "What the hell," he said, and brought out a small elkskin bag. "Take a pinch."

The soap man dipped his fingers in the bag and came up with a small amount of gold dust between thumb and forefinger. He showed it to the buyer, who nodded and put his poke away, frowning at the pile of soap. Finally he selected a bar and tore off the paper. As Slocum expected, there was the flash of specie inside.

A sudden excited murmur ran through the crowd, and Slocum was about to move out of the way of the rush when the dandy in front of him spoke up.

"Now wait a minute," he said in injured tones. "This same fellow was here last night."

The press of buyers halted for the moment. The pitchman turned his watery eyes on the dandy and said, "You'll keep your mouth shut if you know what's good for you."

Slocum saw the menace in those eyes. The young man in front of him apparently did not. "But it's not right," he said. "You're taking their money under false—"

"Not another word," said the pitchman, advancing on the dandy.

"But I must, sir. This other fellow is obviously a shill. He also bought a bar last night, you see, and found—"

The young man never finished the sentence. He was turning to explain himself to the others in the crowd and didn't see the pitchman draw a knife from beneath his vest. The young man only felt the blade of the knife slice through his fine cotton shirt and plunge deep into his belly. He looked down in time to see the knife being withdrawn. He heard the pitchman growl, "God damn it, pilgrim, I *warned* you." And then he stumbled back into Slocum's arms and slid slowly to the ground. With both hands gripping the wound he looked up at the pitchman, who had retreated apparently to watch him die—or to watch developments. No one in the crowd had moved. Now the young man saw Slocum.

"Has he killed me, sir?"

Slocum wanted to kick somebody. He wanted to yell at the kid to stop calling him "sir." Instead he knelt down to look at the wound.

"Yeah, I'm afraid so," he said. "Unless you were hiding your kidney in a safe place. It'll be a few minutes, probably. Anyone you want notified back in the States?"

The boy's eyes shone with tears. "I don't understand," he said. "What did I do wrong?"

"It's just where you are, son. People here are expected to take care of themselves."

"You mean if a man wants to be a sucker, I shouldn't open my mouth?"

Slocum glanced at the harsh faces looking on and he almost smiled, until he turned angry with the realization that none of these men would be grateful for what the boy had tried to do. "That's about it," he said shortly.

The boy flinched in pain. "I could understand a slap on the face, or even a beating."

"Where are you from?"

"Philadelphia."

"There's plenty of law in Philadelphia, son."

The young man glanced at the pitchman, who was scowling back with no other expression in his watery eyes. "You mean he'll get away with this?"

"Oh shit!" said Slocum, and closed his eyes.

"Will he?"

"There'll be a miners' court in the morning. That's the only law here. But since there's no jail, the only charges they'd ever convict on are hanging offenses. This ain't one of 'em."

"But he killed me!" said the man, and for some reason Slocum noticed that he was still clutching the black cane beside him, the other end trembling in the dirt of the street.

"Yeah, but you were interfering with the man's game—"

"You mean his thievery."

"I'll give you that. But I'm talking about how it is out here. The worst that can happen is they'll run him out of town." The stricken look in the young man's brown eyes made Slocum wish he could say something more. He shrugged. "There is a chance some real law will arrest him somewhere else—like they did Jack McCall."

"The man who killed Hickock?" said the man in horror. "You mean they didn't hang him even for *that?*"

"McCall claimed Hickock had killed his brother."

"Oh."

"But I hear a federal marshal picked him up down south somewhere. He may be hung in Yankton."

The young man looked at his murderer, and his eyelids wavered for a moment before he looked back at Slocum. "May I ask your name, sir."

"John Slocum."

"Mr. Slocum—" His body convulsed in pain. "Mr. Slocum,

will you kill that man for me."

Slocum smiled up at the pitchman, who suddenly looked nervous. "I'll think about it," Slocum said.

The pitchman started to say something, and Slocum told him to shut up.

"I can pay," whispered the boy. He brought a long billfold from inside his gray coat and feebly held it up to Slocum. "Take whatever seems fair," he said, "and please send the rest to my fiancée. Would you do me that kindness, sir?"

"*Damn* it, boy. You should have learned more about the West before you came out here."

The boy almost smiled, or would have if he could. "Some of us must always learn the hard way. Sometimes we learn too late."

Slocum took the billfold. It was a light tan color, and it felt like a fine grade of pigskin. "What's to prevent me from keeping everything?" he asked.

The boy glanced about at the other faces. "What are my choices? I will ask for your word, however. These are hard times in the East. My fiancée will be much better off . . . she will *need* this money, Mr. Slocum. Financial security is the very reason I came to this godforsaken place. I will die much more peacefully knowing I have your word."

"Yeah, you got it. Who should I send it to?"

"All the information you need is in that pocketbook. I am very grateful, Mr. Slocum, but I have—" The boy writhed on the ground. "Oh Lord!" he cried. And then, softly but urgently: "I have one more request. Please don't tell her how foolishly I died. A soap salesman! Please don't tell?"

"Son," said Slocum, "I can truly tell you I've never seen a man go better. Don't worry. I'll make it right."

With that Slocum looked up at the pitchman, and something that fellow saw in Slocum's eyes made him raise his knife a little higher. "You wouldn't . . ." he said.

"Thank you," murmured the boy. "You're a good man."

Slocum kept his eyes on the pitchman and the tip of the bloody knife hovering between them. "I wouldn't what?" he said. "Kill you? That would be murder."

Slocum looked at the boy. His eyes were closed. There was

no heartbeat in his chest. Slocum slid the tan billfold into a pocket of his own coat and stared at the boy for what seemed like a long time.

The raucous noise around him, however, slowly intruded on Slocum's reverie. He heard the pounding of hammers and the plodding of hooves and all the other sounds of a town being built almost overnight. He heard them because in his immediate circle there was the stillness of a deathwatch. Slocum gradually realized that all eyes were on him. They had been for perhaps a minute or two. Everyone knew the boy was dead. His body could wait a while for disposition. The only question now was what the big stranger with the green eyes would do. Quickly he glanced over their heads, above the false fronts of the saloons and gambling parlors, as if he wished he could be free of everything around him. He saw the outcroppings of layered sandstone and the small patches of remaining spruce high up on the hill. The topmost trees were bathed in the last golden light from the sun. In the gulch it would get dark very quickly now.

Slocum's gaze dropped suddenly to the unkempt con man in front of him.

"You told him yourself," said the con man. "He was fixin' to spoil my game. I had a right—"

Slocum stood up. "Sure, you had a right. What's his life worth compared to your soap here?"

The salesman kept his knife partly raised, smart enough at least to distrust the words he was hearing.

Slocum fished in the pocket of his trousers and brought out four double eagles. He glanced down at them for a moment, and then again at the pitchman. "I'll tell you what, mister gambling man, let's see how you do when we raise the stakes."

"Hey, I ain't no gambler."

"Sure you are. When you're the house." Slocum slammed the double eagles on the tailgate so hard the con man winced and stepped back. "But I'm the house now, mister gambling man. I just bought every bar of soap on this wagon. And here's my bet. This eighty dollars against your life says I don't find another gold certificate in this whole goddamned pile."

The con man looked at the rough men around him and tried

to hold his panic. "You callin' me a cheat?" he said.

"Yeah."

There was a restless stir of anticipation in the crowd, but barely a sound. Little more than a murmur. The soap man heard it and licked his lips. "I ought to gut you right now," he said.

"Go ahead." When the knife didn't move Slocum reached for the nearest bar of soap and slowly stripped away the brown paper that covered it. The yellowish tint of the soap was even darker in the deepening dusk. He let the paper and the soap fall into the dirt, beside the dead boy, and reached for a second bar.

"You're gonna open three hundred bars of soap?" sneered the con man.

Slocum reached for a third bar.

"You'll probably keep the kid's money anyway, mister. You can't kid me."

Slocum picked up a bar in each hand and tossed one to the Irishman who'd made the crack about expensive baths. They opened the packages in unison and let the soap and paper fall into the street, Slocum's eyes never leaving the con man's face.

"It's a waste," the man said. "All my soap!"

"It's mine now," said Slocum. "You will be too in a few more minutes."

Another member of the crowd reached for a bar of soap and unwrapped it, holding up the paper and the bar before letting them fall. Two more men did the same, then two more.

The pitchman tried to back farther away. He met a wall of hard-muscled bodies. "You said you wouldn't kill me," he cried.

"No," said Slocum, "I only said it would be illegal."

The mounds of paper and soap were growing, higher now than the boy's body. Their former owner looked as if he would cry. "This isn't fair," he said. "You can't do this to me."

Slocum let go of another bar of soap. "I told you I was the house, mister gambling man."

"Stop calling me that."

Slocum only stared back at him, the hint of a smile playing on his lips. The smile made him seem relaxed, but he knew and understood desperate men. He tried to guess, as something of a game, when it would come. He unwrapped a bar and let it go, and had to reach slightly for the next one.

The soap man thought he saw his chance and lunged for Slocum's ribs. He also thought he was fast with the knife, but he never touched his target. Slocum's arm whipped back and parried the thrust, striking so hard that the soap man's knife arm went numb. Slocum whirled around and brought his other hand into the soap man's gut, knocking the wind from him, and before he could fall Slocum hit him with a great roundhouse on the chin that broke his jaw. The man felt the splintering of bone beneath his cheek and was instantly sick with blinding pain. He didn't feel the knife being kicked from his hand. He almost didn't feel Slocum's boot crashing down on his arm, breaking the bone in two.

Any of the watchers in the crowd who might have turned away for a moment would have missed the fight. It was over that fast. But there wasn't any disappointment among them. They stared at the grim John Slocum with a touch of awe, knowing they had seen a rare demonstration. Here was a man to be remembered, and they had actually watched him in action. It would be almost as good a story as seeing Hickock gunned down—and they wouldn't even have to make it up.

Slocum wasn't aware of the mood in the crowd. He was looking at the pitchman writhing on the ground, at first with the wish that he could find any excuse to kill him, then with a combination of pity and disgust. He turned away and scraped his gold coins off the tailgate—he figured he'd come close enough to winning the bet—and walked away from the scene. The men in the crowd respectfully made a path for him, although he wasn't aware of its meaning. If he'd known, he wouldn't have cared.

As he walked away Slocum felt a prickly sensation in his back, along his spine, and he thought: I shouldn't have left that man alive.

2

Later, with time for sober reflection, John Slocum understood that the woman had deliberately picked him out of the boisterous hell-raisers jamming the saloon of the Gem Theater where she worked. The woman had a need, and Slocum would look like the kind of man she had in mind: obviously a drifter, yet several cuts above the common herd and a man who could take care of himself. She saw the bright, dangerous flash in his green eyes, the hard set of his face, the lean and muscled body that was coiled for action even while he leaned casually against the bar. She may have sensed a kind of ferocity that lingered in Slocum, although she probably didn't know yet of the con man and the soap and the beating Slocum had delivered less than an hour before. She may, however, have seen the bruised and swollen knuckles on the hand in which he held his shot glass. She stared at Slocum quite boldly until—finally—he glanced her way, and then she quickly averted her eyes as if embarrassed.

Slocum smiled. His first night back in Deadwood had so far been a disaster, but now it was looking better. The blonde giving him the once-over was barely twenty years old, with the kind of soft pale skin that he ached to touch. Her hair was a honey-colored gold, cascading over her shoulders in luxurious curls and just long enough to touch her breasts where they disappeared beneath the taut fabric of her dress.

It would cost him something. He was north of the deadline, after all, Deadwood's land of saloons and brothels and the "upstairs girls" who worked them. No matter where you looked in this part of the gulch you'd find only one kind of woman.

9

The other kind never crossed the deadline. They attended church socials and entertained their beaus in the parlor and eventually married. Slocum shuddered. The women of the badlands, he thought, simply demanded their money up front.

Later he would smile sadly and say, "If only I'd known what the cost would be."

He sipped his whiskey and admired the blonde, content for the moment to listen to the music and the shouts of laughter echoing from the burlap-covered walls. The burlap had been hung to catch the sap still running from the new-sawed boards— a mark of the freshness and hurry in this exploding gold camp. Slocum could appreciate the solitude of the long days and nights on the trail he'd just traveled, but he also enjoyed the sight of a hundred lonely and work-hardened miners letting loose on the dance floor, whirling the girls in dizzying loops and then holding them close.

Until they ran out of gold dust, that is.

Then a couple of burly men with cruel-looking faces would appear to make sure the fun-lovers caused no trouble as they were being led away from all the joys of a good dance hall. They didn't always want to go peacefully.

That wouldn't be a problem for Slocum, not after his most recent cattle venture south of the border. It wasn't something he'd want to tell his mother about—if she were still alive— but he had survived a stampede, a flood, and two shifty partners with enough money to live out the rest of the winter just over the border. A couple of gents had tried to take it away from him at Mesilla, a matter of poor judgment that had led them to early graves. A few cardsharps had tried to acquire whatever was left by the time he reached Albuquerque and Denver, following the retreating winter snows.

Slocum had taught the cardsharps humility, and he gave expensive lessons. In Cheyenne he was able to buy a fine pair of the little spotted ponies that the Nez Percé raised over on the far side of the Rockies. Those rugged horses were sure-footed in the mountains and long-winded on the trail. He made certain both horses were saddle broke, in case the one he was riding ever went down, but he knew one of them would be carrying the usual prospector's pack of shovel, pan, and pick.

Slocum had decided it was about time to see if he could make something for himself out of the Black Hills gold rush he kept hearing about. He'd tried to fight it, wanting the freedom to wander, but he'd caught the lust for the kind of wealth you can dig out of the ground. He'd missed the big rushes in California and Montana and Idaho, but now he finally knew why they called it gold fever. It *was* a fever. The desire to find the stuff burned somewhere deep inside you. You could think about very little else. In Cheyenne Slocum had met a red-headed whore he knew he wouldn't soon forget who had offered to stay with him for a few weeks—in fact had pleaded with him. But he could only think of all the other men heading north before him, knowing they'd have first crack at finding whatever gold was left. He tried to tell himself it didn't matter, that he should enjoy what he already had in the woman beside him, but after only two nights he assembled his gear. The next morning he slipped out of town and headed for the Platte River, crossing on a crisp day in late April, trying not to remember the tears he'd left behind.

The four double eagles he'd slapped on the tailgate of the soap wagon were all the money he had left when he started from Cheyenne, but he knew it would buy a small piece of a claim if he couldn't find his own. Then he could literally dig up more gold. He also knew most men didn't get rich working a placer claim.

His real goal was to find a promising lead, or shelf of rock, which could be turned into a promising hard-rock mine by some investor or syndicate with the capital to invest in the necessary equipment. That would be the future of the Black Hills, once the placer claims were worked out. Slocum had carefully studied his course of action through the winter. He knew the smart thing to do would be to gamble on finding a hard-rock claim, working it long enough to show its promise, then selling it off to the investors he knew were coming, keeping a percentage of the profits. That way the money would keep flowing to him as long as he lived. And that was the fever that burned inside him, the vision of never having to worry about money again. He'd never have to mess with any damn cows or cow thieves, or the law for that matter. He could go wherever he damn pleased and, more important, do whatever he wanted once he got there.

The girl with the honey-colored hair caught his eye a second time, over the shoulder of a lanky youngster who was drunkenly rocking her back and forth in something that looked like a dance. Slocum smiled again and lifted his glass in silent salute. The woman offered him a shy smile in return. Slocum bought tickets from the bartender—two bits per dance—and waited for the piano player to finish his tune. When the boy stumbled off, Slocum made his way toward the woman, other men instinctively backing away from the tall stranger so that he always had a path through the crowd. The blonde cocked her head a little as she noticed that, and Slocum saw her glance briefly at the well-worn Colt Navy on his hip before her laughing eyes locked on his.

"So you know how to dance," she said.

"Best not jump to conclusions." He gave her a ticket and a wolfish grin. "But let's find out."

She slipped into his arms, and the warmth of her body made Slocum dizzy for a moment—the touch of her hand, the feel of her hair against his cheek, the smell of her perfume. You could try to remember what a woman was like during those hours on the trail, but you'd always be surprised at how pale the memory was.

"I can see I didn't buy enough tickets," Slocum yelled over the noise. "How many dances do you have left tonight?"

The girl laughed, a soft sound that seemed to mingle with the piano chords. "Probably more than you can afford, but thank you for the compliment."

Slocum thought of the dead man's pocketbook in his coat, and some of the joy went out of him. He had never bothered to look inside, and now he wondered how much, if anything, it contained. Slocum rejected any idea of keeping the man's money. He had given his word. He also figured a man who died with that kind of grace deserved to have his final wishes carried out.

"If the night gets that long," he said to the girl, "it must be pretty rough on your feet."

She pulled back to take a look at his face. "The men don't usually care about me in that way. Thanks, stranger."

Slocum shrugged. "Is it rough?"

"I'm not supposed to let it show—"

"But?"

"Oh Lord," said the girl. "If only the miners knew how easy they had it!"

"That's sure saying something."

"But it's wonderful with a man who knows how to dance." She laughed. "And I was right the first time about that."

"About what?"

"You do know how to dance. Do you have a name, stranger?"

"John Slocum."

"Hello, John. I'm Merry Atword."

"Mary?"

"No, Merry. I was a Christmas baby."

"Then I'll come back for a special dance on Christmas."

The girl lost her smile for a moment and missed a beat of the music. "That would be nice," she said distantly, and then she was smiling again, with something like a glint in her eyes. "I bet you can do other things well besides dance."

Slocum smiled back. "I'd hate to be immodest."

"You might be the only man in the gulch who feels that way."

"Hunting gold is a young man's game, Merry, and young men are usually pretty full of themselves."

"Is that the voice of experience?"

"Sure," said Slocum with a laugh. "I see it all around me."

"I don't recall seeing you—before tonight, I mean."

"Just got in."

"To seek your fortune?"

"I think a few thousand fellows have beaten me to it. To the gold itself, at least."

The woman nodded again, watching Slocum, too well-mannered to press for details. The song ended and the girl looked disappointed until Slocum produced another ticket. The next piece was a slow waltz, and Slocum found that Merry Atwood had a natural grace as they glided smoothly together over the floor. But she seemed to trip and reached down as if to adjust her shoe, except that when she brought her hand back up she brushed very gently across the front of Slocum's trousers. He was instantly erect. Merry held her body close as they danced.

They continued to move in unison, but her body gyrated at the same time. It was a subtle movement, but the effect of her belly rubbing Slocum's erection was not. He squirmed and hitched up his pants, and once again he heard her soft laughter. It was muffled against his shoulder.

"I can't help wondering," Slocum said aloud. "I can't help wondering if it's *right* to dance the night away like this. It's important not to waste time, you know."

Merry Atwood pulled away to look up into his eyes, apparently very serious. "Why, John, what else is there?"

Slocum shrugged, and his eyes wandered over the dancers jamming the floor. "I don't know. Lot's of things. We could be . . . playing cards, for example."

"Of course!"

Merry laughed, breaking off in the middle of the dance to head for the bar, Slocum staring after her. She spoke to one of the bartenders, who handed her a pack of cards and watched her walk back to Slocum. She grabbed his hand on the way by and almost towed him toward a small door in the back wall. When she opened it Slocum could see a long dim hallway and perhaps five or six more doors on each side.

Slocum glanced back one more time to see that the bartender was still staring at them. He had both hands flat on the bar and his mouth wide open.

Even above all the noise in the place, the bartender heard a loud laugh as the green-eyed stranger closed the door behind him.

3

Slocum followed Merry down the dim hallway, listening to sounds coming from behind the closed doors. Groans. Muttered curses. The steady, rhythmic crunching of a straw mattress. "Must be some other cardplayers back here," he whispered. "Should we ask them to join us?"

Merry glanced up at him as she paused before one of the rooms, and it was a shy look again, with a quick, uncertain smile. "Let's play one game at a time."

The room wasn't much bigger than a closet, just big enough for a bed and a nightstand that held a bowl of water and a couple of candles. A piece of rough print fabric covered the one window, which was closed, leaving the air with the close, musky smell of sex. Other people's sex.

Slocum took the pack of cards from Merry's hand and put them on the nightstand. "Let's go to my hotel room," he said.

Merry sat on the bed. "I can't, John."

"Why not? I'll just pay—"

"House rules," Merry said shortly. "No exceptions."

"I'll make it worth their while."

The girl seemed to think about something for a moment, then she shook her head. "Really, John. They mean no exceptions."

"But why?"

"I can't tell you, so please don't ask." She was sitting in front of him, and with a tentative, unsure motion she placed one hand directly on the bulge in Slocum's pants. She tried out a smile and said, "I can only think of one thing to do now."

The girl unbuckled Slocum's gunbelt and hung it from a sturdy hook in the wall over the bed, then she unbuttoned his

15

trousers and pulled them to his ankles. Slocum's breath was a rough sound in his throat. He felt a vague discomfort, a sense of alarm deep within his mind, but the voice that told him something was wrong got weaker and weaker as Merry held him in both her hands and kissed his full length.

Merry was still sitting on the bed directly in front of Slocum, who was still standing. He was grinning in a way that made his jaws ache. Merry let him brush her cheek, then filled her mouth with him. She was slow, deliberate, teasing, her lips sliding softly up and down. Slocum leaned against the wall and wrapped his fingers in the soft curls of Merry's hair. After a while he started to shrug off his coat but gave up, needing all his concentration to keep it from ending too soon.

"If this is a game," he murmured, "I think you have the upper hand."

She pulled away, the delicate white fingers of one hand still holding him. "Are you happy, John?"

"I'm not sure that's the word."

"What is the matter?"

"Nothing! Except that I feel like I've spent a week in the desert and now I'm being offered cool spring water—just one drop at a time."

Merry stood up and unhooked her dress. She let it fall to the the floor around her feet. Her movements were all slow and deliberate, more calculated then sensual. But her body seemed to have its own glow in the light from the sputtering candles, and that was all Slocum could see. He never took his eyes away from her as he kicked off his boots and the bunched-up trousers. He pulled off his coat and his shirt and let them fall to the floor as well.

"You surely are a vision," he said.

The girl blushed and looked down at herself for a moment, at the high round breasts with the small pink nipples, and her arms started to move as if to cover herself. But they stayed at her side, and Merry Atwood met Slocum's eyes. "It's all yours, John. And no one's saying you have to take it a drop at a time."

Slocum had finished undressing. He took one last longing look at her and then wrapped her in his arms, folding his hands over her bottom, lifting her so that they tumbled together onto the bed. He was on top, moving until he found her and slipped inside. He plunged as deep as he could, moving slowly, savoring and shivering with every sweet sensation. "The problem is," he whispered, "once you've had your fill the water doesn't taste as good."

Merry kissed his ear. "You'll be thirsty again."

She followed his rhythm as surely as she had followed his lead on the dance floor, moving her hips up to meet his thrusts and then swinging down and away, but still with the same cool sense of . . . what? Slocum was distracted by trying to find the word. Maybe it was craftsmanship. He found now that he was holding himself back, curious, playing a waiting game. The long strokes continued, and suddenly he felt the girl's hot breath in his ear. Now they were together. He felt her shudder, felt her fingers digging into his back. He heard her breathing come in shorter and shorter gasps. Then she arched her back and he was shooting into her while she writhed beneath him, crying out. They gripped each other and slowly relaxed, taking in great gulps of air and grinning foolishly at one another. He touched her cheek, kissed her forehead. She brushed the black matted hair out of his eyes, and she looked surprised.

"You waited for me," she said with a touch of wonder. "You were really thinking about *me*, weren't you? And I don't even think you've had it for a while, have you?"

"A hundred years!" Slocum breathed. "And never like this."

"Liar!" she said with a giggle. She kissed his neck, using tongue and lips in a way that gave Slocum chills from scalp to toe. She seemed so young to know so much, Slocum thought. They kissed for a long moment, Slocum letting the palms of his hands brush over Merry's breasts. She took his hands in hers and looked at them, then at Slocum.

"Would you want me again?" she asked, more a plea than an offer. "I mean, anytime you wanted? Wherever you went?"

The woman's voice tugged at Slocum's heart. "What'll it cost me?" he said gruffly.

"It isn't money I need, John—"

"What else is there?"

"—I have to get out of here."

"So? The stage runs Thursday and Saturday, doesn't it? Tonight's Wednesday, isn't it? Just get on the damn thing tomorrow and go wherever you want to go."

"If only I *could*." She covered her mouth and glanced fearfully toward the door. Slocum could see no hint of artificial theatrics. "Do you have any idea how I got here?" she whispered.

Slocum shook his head.

"The owner himself came to my town. In Ohio. His name's Al Swearingen, and he advertized for young ladies to work in the hotels up here, and with some of the better families."

"And you fell for it?"

"That tells me you haven't met Mr. Al Swearingen. He is a smooth article, that man. And of course there hasn't been much work back in the States since the panic, not enough for my father to—" Merry's voice faded, and she looked off toward the fabric-covered window. "Anyway, we'd heard all the stories of the fabulous fortunes being made up here. It seemed to be a dream come true! A chance to meet the rich mine owners and see some of the excitement—and I hoped to send some money back to my family."

"This Swearingen holds your money?"

"Of course. That's how he keeps us from running away. He says he's saving it for us."

"At least you're meeting people, seeing the excitement."

Merry's eyes wavered and she seemed shaken, perhaps wondering if she'd made a mistake. "When was the last time you saw a whore that was over twenty-five?" she said.

Slocum shrugged.

"Ever?"

"One or two."

"The ones who give up, or like the life, sure. You know how the rest of us die?"

Slocum looked down at Merry's hands, still clutching his own fingers.

"Sometimes it's laudanum," Merry whispered harshly, "because they can't bear the idea of leaving a mark on their bodies. Sometimes it's the little gun, if they want it over with. It's happened right here"—she pointed down to the bed or perhaps the building itself—"right here, twice in the last three months. Good girls, or girls who used to be good, and their families will never see them again. The families get a death certificate that says heart failure, signed by Mr. Swearingen's doctor."

Slocum squirmed.

"It's our only escape. If we do try to get away, we're followed and brought back for a beating. Dear God—if only I could be ugly."

"Now look, Merry—"

"But I'm not vain. I think I'd use a gun. What do you think, John? In the heart?" She moved her finger from her chest to her temple. "Or would it be faster and safer in the brain?" Her eyes were shining in the candlelight. "I don't need money, John. I need *you.*"

"To help you get out of Deadwood."

"And stay out."

"To escape being a whore."

"That's right."

"So you're offering yourself as payment," Slocum said. "I don't see the difference."

"It's all I *have!*" Merry leaned back against the wall, her eyes hard and contemptuous. "It's all I have, and I know it wouldn't last long anyway. I can see you're the type of man who'd get tired of me and want to move on to something different. Then I could go home and try to start over."

"You think you've got me figured."

"Well enough."

Slocum shrugged, thinking she was probably right.

Merry glanced toward the noise coming from the saloon. "You didn't see Sir Galahad out there, did you?"

"Who?"

"Some knight in shining armor who'd be willing to rescue me with no thought of return?"

"No," Slocum admitted. "I'd say they got other things on their minds."

The girl said nothing. She was breathing hard, for the moment unconscious of her body. Her breasts and thighs still gleamed with sweat in the light of the candles.

"Do you know what you're asking me to do?" Slocum said.

He sat on the edge of the bed, thinking it over. The venture would cut into the little working capital he had left, and even if he did make it back to Deadwood in good health he'd have made an enemy of Al Swearingen. He thought of the thousands of prospectors combing every gully and rock face, and the odds decreasing with each passing day that he could find something for himself. On the other hand, when Slocum tried to think about walking out on the girl, he knew it would be impossible. That wasn't the way Slocum was built.

"I'll do it," Slocum said finally. "I'll get you out of here. But it can't be tonight."

"Please, John. I don't know that I can stand it any longer."

"Sure you can. You'll have to. I'm sorry, Merry, but I've got business that can't wait." With the relief of making his decision, Slocum suddenly craved one of the fine Havanas he'd bought in Cheyenne. He leaned down to dig through the pockets of his coat. "Give me a couple of weeks," he said. "Three at the most. Then I'll come back for you."

"Sure you will."

Slocum had found his Havanas, but he was still off balance, leaning far over the bed, and a crucial moment passed before he understood the dry rustle of the girl's voice. That's when the whisper of metal on leather made sense, but it was already too late. In sitting up he only leaned into the blow from his own gun. He twisted as he began to fall, and through a haze he saw Merry holding the barrel of the gun with both hands. Her arms were raised to strike again if necessary.

It wasn't necessary.

4

Slocum woke up to find himself hog-tied, his hands and feet bound by a rope that stretched up to a hook screwed solidly into the wall. His mouth was full of as much of his own shirt as Merry Atwood had been able to cram in, secured by his own bandanna knotted behind one ear. He struggled briefly before he understood how hopeless it was, a black fury building inside him. The girl was still in the room, once again wearing her dress. She'd stopped searching his clothes long enough to watch him struggle.

"I should have known," she said bitterly. "I thought you might be a little different, but I won't make that mistake again. You trust a man and you're only asking for trouble." She glared at Slocum as if daring him to deny it.

He wanted to, but he could hardly get the words out. And the more he thought about it, the more he thought she'd probably be safer with that attitude.

Merry found the double eagles and jiggled them in her palm, letting the candlelight play on their dull yellow surfaces before she put them on the nightstand. In Slocum's coat she found the dead pilgrim's wallet and flipped it open. She and Slocum both saw the embossed calling card inside, and Merry read it aloud.

"Mr. James Q. Eastman, Esquire, of Philadelphia," she said, and looked scornfully at Slocum. "Well now, mister, you are either very good at impersonating a typical western hardcase, or you are a good pickpocket and thief."

Slocum shook his head.

"Your denial is noted," said the girl. "And ignored, of course." She dipped her fingers into a compartment and ex-

21

tracted a thick sheaf of gold certificates that made Slocum's eyes bulge. She counted silently and when she was done she murmured the total with a touch of awe. "One thousand three hundred and thirty-two dollars! At least you pick your victims well, Mr. Slocum."

Again he shook his head. The girl frowned.

"I wish I had the time and ability to discover if Mr. Eastman is still in the gulch," she said aloud, gazing toward the window. "I suppose I could be considered an accessory." She offered Slocum a troubled, speculative look before she made a decision. "I have no choice but to flee," she said. "If I am found, then Mr. Eastman shall surely lose his money to Mr. Al Swearingen. Once I am home I can take steps to return this man's pocketbook." One more bitter look at Slocum. "If I feel he deserves the kindness."

Slocum could sympathize with her bitterness, but he also didn't like paying for the sins of the Gem Theater and its owner.

He never had a chance to talk about fair play. Merry scooped up Slocum's double eagles from the little table and slipped them into the wallet, which she hid somewhere beneath her dress. She then made a final inspection of her appearance and disappeared for the rest of the night. Slocum struggled against the rope for a while, and he tried to sleep for a while. Equally fruitless. Periodically he rocked back and forth on his belly to keep the blood flowing to his elevated hands and feet, but he had to be careful of splinters in his exposed flesh. He was also careful not to crush his organ against the rough wooden floor. He listened longingly to the music and laughter as it slowly ebbed into the early morning.

And he planned. The planning helped him pass the hours and forget the pain in his neck and legs.

The music had nearly stopped when Merry came back, looking weary and sad and disgusted. She stared down at Slocum and thanked him, without meaning it. He wanted to warn her that she should get as far away from him as possible.

She had to crawl on the bed to get by him, and she made sure Slocum was treated to no more a view of her body than necessary. He watched her sit on the end of the bed and produce the wallet from its hiding place long enough to extract a few bills. With the bills folded tightly in her hand she suddenly stopped to stare at Slocum with troubled eyes for a long minute.

"There's always the chance," she said, "that you meant what you told me."

Slocum nodded slowly, emphatically.

Another minute went by. Then the girl opened the wallet again and dug out one of the double eagles. "I can't leave you with nothing," she said. She tossed the coin back onto the little table and moved decisively toward the window. She pushed the fabric aside and threw it open, but paused with one leg over the sill. She was looking back at Slocum.

"If you did," she said, "then I'm doing a terrible thing to you."

Slocum nodded again.

"I'm sorry, John, but I couldn't take the chance. You have to understand. I'm trying to save my *life*." She held his eyes for another long moment, and Slocum realized he did understand. He never placed much trust in other people himself, and he would probably have been doing just what Merry was.

The girl suddenly shook her head and spoke from the harshness of her experience. "Life sure sucks sometimes."

Slocum couldn't have agreed more as he watched her disappear through the window with most of the money he had left.

5

The Gem Theater was quiet for about two hours, but for John Slocum it seemed a much longer time than that before he heard someone walking in the hall. He had already managed to get closer to the door, and now he rammed it with his head, grunting as loud as he could through the gag. It made him furious to feel so foolish—to feel even more foolish when the door was opened by a short, plumpish man whose expression deepened into sorrow when he saw Slocum naked and shivering, trussed up on the floor of the little room.

"Oh, but this is terrible;" said the man, and his head disappeared behind the door. "Butcher!" he shouted, then came back into the room. He frowned and shook his head, jiggling the folds of flesh beneath his chin. "I can't tell you, sir, how sorry I am that you have been victimized by that little tramp." One of the evil-looking men who worked the saloon appeared in the doorway. "Release this man at once, Butcher."

"Right away, Mr. Swearingen."

The man named Butcher pulled a seven-inch knife from a sheath in his belt and cut the ropes between ankles and wrists. Slocum's legs flopped nervelessly to the floor, and Swearingen sat on the bed, rubbing his hands together. "I try to weed out the bad ones," he said. "But as you can see, there is always a risk."

"And a risk in being the customer," said Slocum, the spit-soaked shirt pulled from his mouth. "I should have been more careful. So you're Al Swearingen."

The man give him a closer look. "Yes. And you are..."

24

"John Slocum." He felt sensation returning to his arms and legs. Butcher was sawing at the remaining knots.

"Mr. Slocum!" said Swearingen. "What a pleasure to make your acquaintance, even if it is under these sad circumstances."

Slocum eyed the plump little man.

"Surely you must realize," Swearingen said, "that by now half of Deadwood knows of last night's incident—and is telling the other half. Why, you are something of a hero."

Butcher had finished his work, and now he straightened up with a sound of disgust. "Hero," he said. "What horseshit. It don't take a hero to blindside a man when he ain't looking."

"Enough," said Swearingen. "This man is our guest."

"He came at me with a knife," Slocum said. "When he thought I wasn't looking."

"So you crushed his arm when he was down, mister hero?"

"See to your duties," Swearingen said harshly. "Either you will obey my orders, or you will work elsewhere."

"Sorry," said Butcher. He straightened his thick shoulders, but his heavy black eyebrows were furrowed over his deep-set eyes. "It's just that Johnny Owens is a friend of mine."

"You ought to watch the company you keep," Slocum said.

"And you ought to watch your mouth, mister hero. Someday it'll get closed for good by someone more your own size."

Slocum and Swearingen both opened their mouths to say something, but before either one could say anything Butcher was on his way to the door. "Don't worry," he said. "I'm leaving."

"Let me apologize again for this terrible ordeal," Swearingen said when he was gone. "Naturally we are at your disposal. A fine breakfast? A bottle of our best whiskey? You name it, sir, and you shall have it!"

"The thing I want most right now is the girl's name, and your best guess on where she's headed."

Slocum was rubbing his hands and feet. When Swearingen didn't answer he glanced up to see a cunning look in the man's eyes. "Her name is Merry Atwood, sir. I believe her home was in Iowa."

"Iowa?" said Slocum, remembering that she had said Ohio.

"Iowa, or perhaps Michigan. Here, let me help you up."

He offered Slocum a lift under one elbow, but it still wasn't enough to keep him from stumbling slightly. He sat at the other end of the bed, breathing hard. "So you think she's going home?"

"They usually do, though I'll try to stop her."

Slocum was surprised by the man's candor. "You will?"

"Of course. She managed to steal some of my money before she left, and I can't let her get away with that."

"Of course," Slocum echoed. He doubted the story, and even if it were true, it was probably only the money she had coming.

"If I understand your intentions," Swearingen said thoughtfully, "I know something that may be of use to you. I have reason to believe that Merry Atwood is on the Cheyenne stage even as we speak."

"Already?"

"It left not more than three quarters of an hour ago. It's how I knew to come looking for you."

"What's how you knew?"

"An informant, sir. A friend of mine who saw her on the stage just as it was leaving town. He rushed to give me the intelligence, and naturally I questioned the stage clerk. It seems he recognized Miss Atwood, and what is more, he remembered that she paid for her ticket with cash."

Swearingen looked at Slocum to see if he understood.

"Which she probably got from me," said Slocum. "Right?" He saw no point in mentioning the dead man from Philadelphia.

"Exactly, sir. There's very little scrip here in the gulch, you see. Everyone pays with dust. That's when I realized that she must have robbed a—a stranger here."

"You almost said tenderfoot, didn't you, Mr. Swearingen?"

"Oh no, sir, I assure you—"

"Didn't you."

"Well . . ." Swearingen shrugged and spread his hands with a disarming smile. "I must confess that was my first hypothesis," Swearingen told Slocum. "But I can see the marks of much experience upon your flesh—the marks of bullet, knife, and whip."

Slocum grinned and reached for his clothes. "That's something other men don't normally get a chance to talk about."

"I'm quite sure. But the point I was coming to, Mr. Slocum, is that perhaps we can join our common interests."

"How?"

"You intend to find Miss Atwood, do you not?"

"If it's the last thing I do."

"Exactly! You bring to the job a determination that would be lacking in anyone I sent after her. And I naturally prefer to keep my staff at full strength."

"Sure," said Slocum. "What would the Gem be without Butcher?"

"He is actually quite useful, sir. And do not underestimate the man."

"Did someone actually give him that name?"

Swearingen laughed. "Only by trade. That's what he used to do in the States. I must say that in my business it's helpful to have men around you who aren't overly squeamish."

"I'll bet," Slocum said. He thought about Butcher getting hold of Merry Atwood, and didn't like what he thought. The owner of the Gem took his silence for indecision, and brought out other arguments for his proposal.

"There is also the fact that it is only our word against hers," Swearingen said. "Since my reputation is, for some reason beyond my comprehension, not among the best here, it would be best to accomplish the whole thing . . . informally."

"I understand," said Slocum, who had arrived at the same conclusions during the night. That is, he had decided that the law would be useless in recovering his money—or the money that he had promised to deliver to Eastman's fiancée.

"Therefore, you see, it would be worth a percentage of the recovery to remain uninvolved."

Swearingen waited while Slocum considered. It didn't take long to realize that he was, in effect, being offered a bonus for a job he planned to do anyway.

"I wouldn't have to bring her back?" Slocum asked.

Swearingen looked shocked. "What would *we* want with her?"

"It's just the money, then."

Swearingen nodded. "Two small pouches of dust, to be

exact. You'll keep twenty percent."

"It's a deal," said Slocum. He figured the agreement would keep Swearingen's men out of his way, and away from Merry.

He could always decide when the time came whether Swearingen deserved to get his money back.

6

The sun was high overhead when Slocum pounded out of the trees onto the Cheyenne-Deadwood stage road thirty-five miles southwest of the gulch. He swung down off his lathered pony to examine the tracks, but there was no sign of freshly disturbed earth. He inhaled deeply, catching no trace of lingering dust in the hot, still air. Slocum looked up the road toward Deadwood for a full minute, and then he grinned. It was not a grin anyone would have enjoyed seeing.

Slocum walked his mount along the road, cooling him down at the same time that he scouted for a good location. A half mile farther the road began a long ascent that leveled out on a blind curve. Slocum stopped and turned toward Deadwood again, preparing himself for the job. There came now the first stirring of his blood, the pulsing that he could feel in his ears. It faded, as it should, and Slocum moved back into the woods to stretch out against a tall pine. He was glad Merry Atwood had also left him his Havanas. He smoked one now, as he waited.

Al Swearingen had supplied him with a detailed description of the shortcut, a tortuous path down Icebox Gulch and then back and forth along Spearfish Creek to Graveyard Springs, up the Long Draw in the heart of the Black Hills. It was rugged, broken country of high granite walls and ponderosa pines mingling with Black Hills spruce. When the wind stirred, it sang in the trees, and when it was still, the cry of piñon jays and kingfishers filled the silence. The warm air carried a soft fragrance unlike any Slocum had ever smelled, and not a single mosquito disturbed his reverie. He rubbed his wrists and ankles

29

and caught himself thinking: If I could ever settle down...

He daydreamed along those lines, and after a time he became aware of the distant thud of hooves and then the jangle of harness as the Concord coach slowed for the grade. When it was closer he could hear the squeak of the leather thorough-braces that carried the body of the coach. Slocum led his horse onto the road and waited quietly behind the saddle, gun drawn, fingers flexing about the butt of the Colt. The sensations rushing through his body were so familiar that they brought images of other battles, other conflicts, until he drove them out to clear his mind.

He knew he would need every instinct at his command.

To stop a stage single-handed was pure cussed foolishness, because no matter how good you were, you couldn't be sure of controlling the entire situation. There were too many people involved—a driver and at least one brave shotgun messenger on top, and as many as nine passengers inside, including gun-handy miners and merchants ready and able to protect their valuables. Slocum wasn't the only veteran of the War Between the States.

But Slocum was too mad to care. And he had the help of Al Swearingen, who had assured him that only one guard rode the stage that day and that the four passengers had appeared fairly harmless. Travelers were already smart enough to carry as little money as possible and to take robberies as a matter of course. That way there was little risk of bloodshed, and little loss.

Slocum's plan worked in steps. With luck he would take care of one problem at a time.

The first thing the driver and guard saw when they rounded the bend, slowed by the long uphill climb, was a big, hard-looking man standing behind his horse, gun arm leveled across the saddle, and not a hint of fear on his face. Their thoughts were the same: Here is a man shielded from harm, whose bullets will go exactly where he wants them to go. The driver, who had a wife in Cheyenne, pulled hard on the reins. The guard decided he would wait for a better opportunity.

Slocum tried to make sure there would be none. "Get down," he ordered the guard, motioning with his Colt. "On your belly, damn it! Driver, keep both hands wrapped in those reins."

Slocum remained in front of the stage, so that any passenger who wanted to try for him would have to lean far out to get a clean shot. "You inside," he yelled. "Come on out here one at a time. The first gun I see means someone dies." They started filing out, two of them looking nervous and two of them looking almost bored. "Line up beside the guard. Keep him company and take a rest."

Four passengers lay beside the guard. They were all men.

"I want everyone," Slocum growled. "Where's the woman?"

"There never was no woman," said the driver.

"Don't give me that shit. I was told there was."

"Look for yourself, mister."

For the first time Slocum confronted the uneasy feeling that had been gnawing at him all morning. There was something far too smooth about Mr. Al Swearingen. Now he felt a renewed stirring of that black rage he knew so well. He walked his horse carefully to the side of the coach. The passengers lay very still on the carpet of brown pine needles beside the road. Slocum looked them over, then looked into the coach. He muttered a string of curses when he saw the empty seats. Either the girl had pulled a fast one, or Swearingen had lied. If Swearingen had lied, then there had to be a reason. He could probably figure it out if he had the time to go back over the last twenty-four hours and fit the events into a logical story. So far he'd been too busy, and this sure as hell was not the time to start.

Slocum turned on the passengers again, thinking about the little bit of gold they'd be carrying—thinking that no matter how little it was, it was more than he had. But it would be his first crime in Dakota. He figured he had a choice between starving or eating well as he turned his back on the hills.

Things couldn't get much worse, he thought.

"There's two barrels of double-ought buck lookin' right at you," said a voice behind him.

Slocum froze.

"Please don't," said the voice. "I'd have to kill you."

Slocum believed the voice. "Shit!" he said, slowly laying his Colt Navy on the pine needles. He stepped away and turned around. The shotgun was there, as advertised, not thirty feet away and in the arms of a sandy-haired character of about forty. Slocum sighted back along the barrels into a pair of cool, watchful blue eyes, and suddenly he shivered. He knew that in his frustration he had come close to making a play.

And to dying.

Just as suddenly Slocum laughed.

"Have you remembered a joke?" said the man with the shotgun.

"A joke on me, I guess. Just a minute ago I was thinking things couldn't get much worse."

The man had a kindly smile. "It's never smart to tempt fate with a dare, my friend. Your troubles are just beginning."

"I see your point," said Slocum. "What now?"

"Gene will see that you're indisposed."

The messenger had already picked himself up and was brushing himself off, the others deciding to remain on the ground just a while longer. The messenger found shackles in the boot of the stage. Slocum let his wrists be cuffed behind him.

"And now you'll be a guest of Harrison, Gilmer, and Salisbury as far as Cheyenne," said the sandy-haired man. "After that it's up to the federal marshal."

"I suppose it's just a small detail, but I didn't actually rob anyone."

The passengers had decided it was safe to stand up, and they watched the little drama intently. They saw the man with the shotgun glance at the guard.

"Claimed he was looking for a woman," the guard said.

The man with the shotgun nodded and looked at Slocum. "Kidnapping is even more serious than robbery."

"I wasn't planning to—"

"Ah, but how do we *know* that?"

Slocum smiled. "Because I have a face you can trust?"

The sandy-haired man shook his head. "You're a cool one, aren't you? Gene, I guess we'll ride along in back for a while."

The guard nodded and climbed into the boot once more. The passengers were already getting back into the coach, murmuring excitedly among themselves.

"At least they'll have stories to tell," Slocum said.

The other man lowered his shotgun and came up beside him. "It's a time and place for stories," he said, "and precious few of them left. They'll have to enjoy it while they can, I'm afraid, because in a few years there won't be any difference between the Black Hills and . . . New Hampshire."

"Sure there will."

"Did you come through Cheyenne on the way here, by any chance? Eleven years old—that's all it is—and you might as well be in Denver."

"Denver ain't so shabby."

"No, I guess not," said the other man wistfully. "It's just not the *same*."

"Maybe you're right," Slocum growled. "Damn it, maybe I just don't want to believe it yet." But he knew the man was right, and he also knew, as crazy as it sounded, that he was looking forward to this ride. It would be a pleasure to talk with a man who took the trouble to think about things.

The coach had pulled out in a cloud of dust, and now Slocum let himself be led to his horse and helped into the saddle. His captor tied his feet beneath the horse's belly, then cut another length of rope to lead Slocum's mount on the trail. The sandy-haired men gave Slocum a puzzled frown.

"You're taking this all rather calmly," he said.

"We have a long way to go."

"Don't expect any chances, mister. Not from me. Nor any hope of leniency."

"I never do." Slocum thought about Merry Atwood and Al Swearingen. "Christ, I only came up this trail yesterday. Nine days of hard riding on a sore ass, and now it looks like I'm going right back where I started from."

"Not to mention what might happen when you get there."

"Yeah, there's that."

The cool blue eyes studied him. "I guess you should have thought about that before you decided to rob the stage."

"Don't play so dumb," Slocum said fiercely. "You sure as hell aren't stupid, and I'm not stupid enough to believe you are."

The blue eyes didn't waver, didn't change expression.

"What kind of self-respecting road agent stands there trying to figure out what to do next? You saw enough to know I was looking for someone."

"Why?"

"None of your goddamned business."

The other man merely shrugged. "I couldn't help noticing your Navy," he said. "Trying to make out like Hickock?"

Slocum laughed. "Look where it got him. No sir, I ain't no Hickock. But we probably started carrying 'em in the same way—during the war."

"And for the same reason?"

"I don't know what Hickock's reasons were," Slocum said carefully.

"He used to say that the first shot was the one that counted—"

"If it goes home."

"—and he thought the Navy the most accurate revolver."

"One of 'em, anyway. Look at the length of that barrel."

"You have a name, mister?"

"John Slocum."

"Now there's a name to reckon with," said the sandy-haired man, looking puzzled and respectful at the same time. "I seem to have heard something about a stabbing last night."

"You and everyone else, I guess. I just happened to be behind the poor bastard."

"And you just happened to buy that fellow's lot of soap? And put his knife arm out of commission?"

"I got mad."

"Then I'm none too happy I was the one who arrested you." The sandy-haired man smiled at Slocum. "Are you mad at me?"

"I might be. If we get all the way to Cheyenne."

"I must say it doesn't make sense, your holding up a stage when you ought to have a considerable amount of money in your pocket. Another man's of course, but just the same . . ."

"You keep thinkin' like that."

"I also must say I never heard your name before this morning. If it's your true name."

"It is. I make an effort to keep it off as many wanted posters as possible. And I haven't ever gone in for advertising myself in the penny dreadfuls."

"Now there's a point in your favor! It's sad enough that the West is disappearing, but when I think of it being remembered that way..."

"Who the hell are you?" Slocum said.

"The name's Horatio Brown."

Slocum shook his head.

"I'm the superintendent for Misters Harrison, Gilmer, and Salisbury."

"Superintendent of the stage line? What are you doing out here?"

"A tour of inspection, you might call it. Now that the Indian pressure is off we've been having some trouble with other kinds of varmints."

"Meaning road agents like me?"

Horatio Brown looked at Slocum with a hint of amusement in his eyes. "I expect that part will get worse before it gets better," he said. "No, I mean stock thieves. I don't want to suggest a new line of work to you, Mr. Slocum, but our need for way stations makes us vulnerable. We have to keep fresh animals every twenty or thirty miles or so along the route, of course, and often in the most isolated and unprotected locations. We've been losing stock at an alarming rate. If the situation isn't changed soon, the replacement costs alone could literally put us out of business. Who was the woman, Mr. Slocum?"

"The woman?"

"You claimed to have been looking for one, I believe."

"Oh yeah. Merry Atwood. She was just a dance hall girl at the Gem."

"It would seem there are plenty of them to go around," Brown said mildly. "Was there any particular reason you stopped the stage at gunpoint for this one?"

Slocum nodded, his mouth turned down in a frown of disgust.

"May I hear the reason?"

"I suppose you have the right. She stole sixty dollars from me, along with that poor pilgrim's pocketbook."

Brown smiled.

"I don't see the humor," Slocum said.

"You will, my friend. You will in time. I think that part of the humor lies in the fact that you haven't been bested many

times in your life. Am I right? I thought so. You generally
come out on top, and yet here you are, almost surely on the
way to a long prison term. All because of this little dance-hall
girl."

"I wasn't paying attention to my instincts. I must be getting
old. But, damn it, Brown, you know I wasn't planning to rob
those people."

"Possibly."

"Then why are you holding me? If you take me all the way
to Cheyenne I'll never see that money again."

Brown stared at Slocum. "Because I couldn't be sure, and
because I might be able to use a man like you."

"Christ, that's what the girl said just before she hit me over
the head with my own gun."

Brown laughed. "Perhaps your mistake was in saying no."

"Are you trying to tell me something, Brown?"

"It's a thought. But we might be able to work out an agreement that would suit us both."

Slocum sighed. "I might as well hear you out."

"In good time."

"Time's a-wasting, man! Let's get on with it."

Brown's expression remained calm. "You made a hasty
decision and look where it got you, my friend. No, this will
take some thought. You must relax and enjoy the scenery. This
is one of the prettiest stretches on the road."

Slocum shook his head and almost smiled. Brown was not
an outwardly hard man, or a flashy one, but he had bottom.
Slocum wasn't so stubborn that he couldn't admire someone
who shared his own stubborn ways.

He knew that when Brown got around to talking, he'd be
listening carefully.

7

Slocum brushed a hovering fly away from his face and rested his forearms on the rough wooden table before him, his jaws going to work on another chunk of gristly beefsteak. Grains of sand grated between his teeth, and his shackles clinked against the tin plate beneath his hands. In the brilliant light of the midday sun he seemed to be staring at the plate, but his every sense was keyed toward escape.

The chance seemed remote, even though Brown and Slocum had made an agreement.

The superintendent's calm blue eyes never strayed far from his prisoner as the two men ate with the other passengers in the front yard of the Deep Springs stage station, about halfway to the southern flank of the Black Hills. The building was behind them, a small, poorly made cabin showing several gaps between the logs, and the coach stood twenty feet in front of them, looking abandoned and a little forlorn without the horses. Or perhaps it was only a reflection of Slocum's mood. It was nearly two o'clock on the afternoon of his misadventure and he was still imprisoned. He'd been allowed to eat with his hands in front of him, but if he was to have even the slightest chance of escaping he would have to make his move very soon, before his hands were once again clamped behind his back.

That was part of the agreement.

"The fellow who runs the place is Bill Rousseau," Brown had said earlier in the afternoon, while they were still on the road. "He's one of my suspects."

"The stationmaster?"

"They need an inside man to keep an eye on our guards, Mr. Slocum. Rousseau seems like a good prospect."

37

"Why?"

Brown had smiled. "He doesn't complain enough. Tending stock is not one of the favorite jobs in this company."

"So you want me to make my try in front of him?"

"It should be a good introduction, don't you think?"

"If he's helping the ones that steal your stock."

Slocum heard a commotion behind him and turned from the dinner table to see a pair of husky grays prancing around the corner of the poor log hut, dwarfing the man who led them. He had shiny black hair and a thick beard of black curls. Bill Rousseau also had a gloomy disposition and an ever-present scowl on his face. He'd said no more than ten words since their arrival. Slocum watched him carefully as he hitched the horses to the stage. Their eyes met and held for a moment.

The superintendent's proposal had been simple enough. He would give Slocum a few days to find the girl and the money, after which Slocum would try to make contact with the gang of stock thieves. He would learn their names, where they operated, and how they unloaded stock. "I want a perfect case," Brown had said. "I want every last man."

"It's not my normal line of work."

"You hardly look the type," Brown had said dryly. "But that's why I think the job suits you so well. If you'd rather take your chances in Cheyenne . . ."

"You're willing to take my word that I'll make the effort?"

"That, and the knowledge that one thousand dollars in reward money can be a powerful incentive."

"I was planning to find a gold mine."

Horatio Brown had looked bemused. "And so are ten thousand others, my friend. Ten may be lucky. A bird in the hand . . ."

The passengers were starting to drift away from the table, to stretch or walk or pay a visit to the smaller house behind the log one. It was almost dark, and the driver and his guard were still resting inside the cabin. Slocum considered various diversions. He thought about tin plates as weapons. He judged distances. And finally he rejected anything complicated. Escape would have to be simple and sudden. And believable. Slocum decided Brown would be most vulnerable when he unlocked the cuffs, and he began to prepare for that moment.

It never came. Brown stood up from the table with an odd glint in his eyes, backing away from Slocum and suggesting that he simply step over the cuffs until they were once again behind him.

Slocum got to his feet. "I don't think I can. I'm too stiff."

"Of course you can. Otherwise I'd have to disturb the guard from his rest."

"You bastard," said Slocum, not entirely for show.

He saw the stationmaster from the corner of his eyes, standing in the doorway of his cabin. He sighed and began to put one foot between his arms, again judging the distance to the spot where Brown stood alert, gun still in a shoulder rig beneath his jacket. As Slocum stepped he also started to lean. It appeared he had lost his balance, falling forward. He hopped once, then put all his strength in the leg still on the ground and pushed off, tucking his head so that he rolled on his neck and shoulders.

"Hey!" Brown yelled.

Slocum heard a shot and felt a bullet burn the calf of his leg while he was still coming around. He couldn't believe it was Brown's gun, but he knew from the direction of the sound that it had to be. He rolled onto his feet in a crouch under Brown's arm and bowled him over. Another shot exploded in his ear. He used his body to pin the superintendent to the ground, twisting around to grab Brown's arm and then his gun before he rolled away. He heard more shots from the cabin and saw the guard firing his revolver from the doorway. Rousseau had disappeared. Slocum put two bullets into the logs beside the guard's head, and threw his manacled arms over Brown's shoulders when the guard ducked away. The guard reappeared with his shotgun, but he saw his boss being hoisted off the ground to provide a shield for Slocum. The guard aimed his shotgun and held the pose, giving Slocum the second chance that day to stare into the barrels of a deadly ten-gauge Greener. *What am I doing wrong?* he thought.

Slocum pulled Brown back toward the boot of the stage and ordered him to unlock the shackles. With one arm free, Slocum felt in the boot for his Colt, knowing there was only one more shell in the revolver he'd taken from Brown. Finally he dragged the superintendent toward the horses tied behind the coach, keeping one nervous eye on the shotgun.

Still holding Brown within the iron grip of his arm, he managed to free both horses. He pulled the reins over the neck of his own pony and transferred his Navy to that hand. "You'd better drop as flat as you can," he whispered to Brown, then fired the last bullet in the borrowed revolver toward the doorway and jumped on the superintendent's horse when the guard ducked back a second time. He was low in the saddle and running the horse like a bat out of hell when he heard and felt the blast of the guard's shotgun. Some of the slugs thudded into the pines beside the road. A few more whistled by to one side and overhead. Slocum automatically tensed his muscles, expecting impact, but he had survived the first volley and was already too far out of sight to worry about another.

8

"That was a neat trick, taking both horses," said Horatio Brown.

"Thanks," said Slocum.

"At first I thought you were just trying to limit pursuit, until we found my horse."

"That sure as hell didn't stop you, did it."

"I gave them the chance to quit."

"Just like you gave me the chance to escape?"

"But I did! I pointed out that you had a durable horse which was relatively fresh—fresher than ours by far—and that the draft horses were hardly built for speed." Brown sighed. "Just remember this if you ever decide to stop a stage again. Our guards don't know when to quit."

"I'll keep that in mind."

The two men saw each other only as dark shapes. It was close to midnight, and they were alone beneath a scrub oak in a draw that ran north and west from Deep Springs Creek. They had met, as agreed on the trail that morning, at an abandoned cabin in the draw. The stage road itself was less than three miles away.

Slocum heard a scratching sound, and a lucifer flared in front of Brown's face, just above the bowl of a pipe. The superintendent was smiling. "Even so, I think we gave you quite a run."

"You got close," Slocum admitted. "Too close for my comfort."

"That's what I figured when we couldn't smell your dust anymore." Brown sucked the flame of the match into the bowl of his pipe, then shook out the match. "You hit for the woods?"

"Yeah."

"We tried to find your trail, of course."

"Even if you had," said Slocum, "your horses wouldn't have followed mine."

"That's one of the Nez Percé ponies, isn't it?"

"Got another one just like it stabled up in Deadwood. At least I hope I do."

"You've certainly earned the right to go and find out. You gave a fine performance, Mr. Slocum."

"Now you're a critic."

"Of course, I had to aim a bit wide to make it look good."

Slocum rubbed his leg. "Not wide enough, damn it. I have to hand it to you, Brown. I never thought you'd be that fast getting your gun out of a shoulder rig."

"Don't forget that I knew you had to do something pretty quick."

"You didn't exactly make it easy on me."

"I was thinking of the audience," Brown said. "I don't see any way Bill Rousseau could suspect a setup, do you?" Brown laughed out loud. "You sure were a sight, Slocum, running off with those horses."

"Oh yeah? Just imagine what a sight I'd have been if that Greener had been better aimed."

"Don't be sore, my friend. I was taking chances too."

"That's your job."

"Yours too, now. And listen." The superintendent was suddenly serious. "Don't take this gang too lightly. The average road agent is nothing more than a fortune hunter down on his luck. But these stock thieves are a different breed. They don't mind killing."

"Neither do I," Slocum said harshly.

"I suppose not."

Slocum realized that Brown felt uncomfortable, and he wondered if it had to do with something that separated the two men. Brown was smart and fast, but he remained civilized in some subtle way that Slocum was not. Slocum felt a moment of regret when he realized the other man thought of him as a natural killer, a kind of savage, and the thought made it harder for him to say what he was about to say. Slocum told himself that the men who could kill let the ones like Brown stay comfortable.

"Anyway," said Slocum, "there's something you oughta know about your man Rousseau. I've seen him before."

Brown caught his breath. "Did he recognize you?"

"I expect."

"Are you saying this will hurt our chances?"

"I doubt it. We shared a cell in El Paso for a day or two."

"I see."

"He thinks I shot a man and took his horse."

"Ah." Brown made a sucking noise, and the tobacco embers glowed in the night.

"Polite of you not to ask," Slocum grunted. "I guess you'll just have to take my word for it that the man needed killing."

"I'm sure," said Brown, sounding as though the words had a bad taste. "What was Rousseau's offense?"

"Just a saloon brawl. Except his name wasn't Rousseau."

"Oh?" said Brown, sounding only vaguely interested.

"Nope. He called himself Chambers at the time."

"Good Lord, man!" Brown jumped to his feet. "Was it Gerry Chambers?"

Slocum thought for a second or two. "Sorry, I can't remember."

"But it must be! I've heard that Bill had a brother."

"Bill who?"

"Sorry, Slocum. The man who seems to run things here, they say his name is Bill Chambers. He's taken to calling himself Persimmon Bill, for some reason."

"Can't you arrest him?"

"Can't lay a hand on the son of a bitch. So far it's all just rumor and guesswork—loose talk—and the man circulates with impunity. One of my own drivers found him loitering about Rousseau's place last month and called him a thief to his face. Stupid thing to do. Lost his temper, I suppose. His companions begged him not to continue that night, but he couldn't back down. He was ambushed not four miles down the road. Shot in the back." Brown paused, and Slocum could see a glow from the bowl of the pipe. "This is the kind of man you are dealing with, Mr. Slocum. I've just heard that he also shot an Army sergeant who tried to arrest him in Wyoming Territory, but it's the same story as my driver. You *know* what happened—but you can't prove a thing. This fellow is a ruthless snake, Mr. Slocum. A charming one, you will find, but that makes him all the more dangerous. He seems to have friends who will protect him."

"You have no idea where he hides?"

"That is what I hope you can discover. It is probably not far from the Springs, but there are a million hiding places in the Black Hills. And, as you no doubt have seen, it is a rugged place for pursuit."

"I've noticed," Slocum said dryly.

"I need one good witness, Mr. Slocum! One man who can tell a judge how the gang operates. When I see Chambers and his gang dangling from the end of a rope, you will receive . . . shall we say, your one thousand dollars?"

"Two thousand sounds a lot nicer."

"You're hardly in a position to bargain."

"Another poster in the post office won't bother me all that much, Brown. A hell of a lot less than maybe getting shot up by a gang of thieves."

There was a silence while the superintendent seemed to be thinking. "All right," he said finally. "It'll certainly be worth that to put the Chambers gang out of commission. But I want them all, Slocum. Every last one."

"I'll do my part. Just see that you do yours."

"Don't worry. Harrison, Gilmer, and Salisbury pays its bills."

Slocum grunted. Then he asked where the superintendent could be located.

"I'll take the next stage down," said Brown. "I'll say I lost your trail completely. I'll await word from you there."

"What name will you use?"

"What's wrong with—oh yes, you did gain some notoriety last night. How does . . . Matthew Ross strike you?"

"They'll have my description, of course."

"I'll confuse the issue, Slocum. No one will know exactly what to believe. But what about Rousseau? Will he know you as John Slocum?

"Not likely."

"Just how many names have you had, Mr. Slocum?"

"Guess I've lost count," he said shortly.

"Well, for now you are Matthew Ross," said Brown, chuckling. "Try not to forget. And in the meantime I'll pay heed to any message I get from JS." Brown took another pull at his pipe. "Tell me something, Mr. Slocum. I saw you hesitate this afternoon, when I had the drop on you, and I've been wondering ever since. Were you going to rob those people?"

Slocum laughed. "Neither one of us will ever know. You never let me decide."

"There is one other thing you should know."

"Yeah?"

"I had a tip that there might be an attempt on the stage today. That's why I was riding outside."

"So?"

"Al Swearingen's the man who gave me the tip."

9

Something about Slocum had changed by the time he reached the top of Strawberry Hill late the next afternoon, and he thought about it as he wove his careful way between the heavy freight wagons making their way down the steep slope. He glanced back occasionally to make sure he wasn't in danger of being run over, but mostly he daydreamed. He had followed this same road through the heart of the Black Hills only two days before, and nothing around him had changed. The tall pines and spruce along the way were the same rich green, the sky overhead just as blue. The rough-looking men along the trail were the same schemers and dreamers, hoping for the rich strike or the lucky break that would be the answer to all their hopes. But he himself was different, as though it was some other man entirely who had ridden down this trail on Slocum's horse. And because this was a feeling that John Slocum didn't understand—because he would need his full concentration for the next few days—Slocum tried to remember that first trip.

Instead he found himself remembering another trip entirely, the return to his family farm after the war. He had barely survived those terrible years of killing, but that was still more than he could say for the rest of his family. In going home he had wanted to put it all behind him. Not that he'd ever truly forget finding the body of his older brother on the field at Gettysburg. He and Robert had dreamed of running the family place together, but when war broke out between the states, young John had been eager to fight. His older brother had gone along only reluctantly—and now he was the one who was dead. Slocum's father had taken a minié ball at Ball Run that removed him from the fighting, but also left him weak. He succumbed to sickness and died while Slocum was mired in the gruesome bloodshed of Kansas. His heartsick mother died not long after, died before the dirt had settled on her husband's grave.

John Slocum had only one thing left in 1866, the good pasturage and fertile bottomland of Slocum's Stand in Calhoun County, Georgia. He went back to the homeplace and the dream he had shared with his brother to rebuild the only home he had ever known.

Fate had other plans. She always did, it seemed. First by way of the war itself, and now by way of one of the carpet-baggers it left behind. He was a judge in the new government who claimed ownership of Slocum's Stand. He'd made up something about nonpayment of taxes, which was a crock, but the judge had the law on his side. Slocum had nothing but a pair of Colt Navies he thought he'd put away forever, and a code of honor that told him the judge and his henchman shouldn't get away with stealing the family land. He killed the judge and his hired gun in a fair fight, knowing even as he watched them die that his act of honor had won him nothing. He would still lose the one thing he had left after the war. He fired the house in which he'd been born, the two barns, even the springhouse, and rode into the West one step ahead of the warrant he knew was coming.

Walking his horse slowly down the road to Deadwood, Slocum suddenly understood what had changed. The man who had ridden this trail two days before had a wild dream about finding a hard-rock mine in a new country where thousands of men were making fresh starts. He had also been riding the long lonely trails for more than ten years now, and sometimes he had wondered about a different life. It was all in how you looked at it. Sure, he had been a free man all that time. And there was nothing sweeter than feeling the call to be somewhere else. You might find yourself scooping brown water out of a mudhole in the Sonoran desert, dreaming of the high mountain meadows in the Wind River Range of Wyoming. Suddenly you'd feel the soaring of your spirit, knowing that all you had to do was turn your pony north. There were new sights and new adventures everywhere you went, not to mention every kind of woman you could imagine.

But sometimes you would pass a little cabin by the road and you would see a man and his wife working side by side in the fields, or you might catch a glimpse of them in front of their fire at night, and you would wonder... It would be a thing you'd think about more and more as you got older. It could sneak up on you when the days got shorter and you started smelling winter in the air. That would be the time to think about a home, wondering if you yourself would ever have one.

Slocum knew that's what had happened. Without realizing it, he'd spent the past winter thinking of coming to the Black Hills never to leave, just as he had gone home to Slocum's Stand to make a life there. But Fate had once again played her hand. Slocum let out a short, bitter laugh over the joke, and he decided he was being warned about something he had learned long ago and was almost in danger of forgetting. He didn't go so far as to give it a name, or think much more about it, but he remembered the first bloody days of the war when he'd seen the death of one friend after another. He remembered how he stopped making friends. He relived his final days at Slocum's Stand, and had a brief sense of the long years since—the years of freedom and drifting. He had been a fighter, living by his wits and reflexes, and his weakness of a few days before— for that is how he viewed it now—had left him vulnerable and soft. He cursed himself for falling prey to the girl and her boss, but he also felt powerful and clearheaded now that he was reminded what kind of life Fate had in store for him. The only thing he cared about anymore was finishing his business with Mr. Al Swearingen.

The stage superintendent's revelation of the night before had been a jolt. But it also clarified many things for Slocum. Swearingen must have been lying about the tip that Merry Atwood was seen on the southbound stage, and the tip itself— combined with informing Horatio Brown—was a clever way to dispose of Slocum. Swearingen must have hoped for a shoot-out and the immediate dispatch of his victim, but an arrest and hanging in Cheyenne would have been damn good enough. Slocum had been doing a lot of thinking about Swearingen, and now he saw him clearly for the dangerous enemy that he was. What he didn't know was whether Merry Atwood had been another of Swearingen's victims or his partner.

The man who sold stage line tickets in the mornings went by the name of Warren Bates. With help from the night clerk Slocum tracked him down to his dinner table in the IXT dining room. Bates was a slow-moving man who kept on eating his stew even when Slocum walked up and waited patiently for recognition. Good manners didn't work, so Slocum pulled out a chair on the other side of the table and sat down. The man he was now facing slowly lifted his square jaw and did absolutely nothing for about the count of ten. Then he said, "The office is still open, mister. It's in the next block, and the fellow who's on duty isn't eating his dinner."

Slocum stared at Bates, genuinely curious. "You're the man I need to see," he said, "and you happen to be right here at the moment, and I can't help it if you're eating. And what the hell makes you so unfriendly?"

"Not a thing, mister. It's just that ten hours a day isn't enough work. I don't get enough characters like you to bother me at dinner and help fill up my day."

"This will be a disappointment, then, because what I need won't take long."

"I'm heartbroken."

"I want to find a good-looking blonde."

"Don't we all. You might try—"

"And you might try to shut up," Slocum snapped. "This is important business, and I'm going to sit here until I'm done no matter how hard you try to offend me, got that? I don't expect to bust out in tears because you're being mean. So answer a question or two and then you can go back to your stew. If it hasn't turned sour on you."

The man's expression didn't change, but he didn't say anything either. Slocum nodded. "We're talking about yesterday morning," he said. "Were there any women on board the stage?"

Slocum saw the faintest narrowing of the man's eyes. "Not when it left Deadwood."

"But a woman did buy a ticket, right?"

"What are you, a husband?"

Slocum laughed despite himself. "Not hardly."

"What then?"

"Does it matter?"

"It does if she missed the stage because she was trying to run away from someone."

Slocum nodded thoughtfully. "I see your point. And I think it's a fine thing, trying to protect a stranger."

The ticket seller kept his eyes on Slocum's face, his own expression never changing while he seemed to be thinking in his slow deliberate way. "Maybe she ain't a stranger," he said.

Slocum grinned. "Of course! You've probably been here all summer, and so has the Gem, and Merry's one of the prettiest girls there."

The ticket seller's expression had turned ugly. "None of your damn business," he said.

Slocum turned serious. "Consider this, then. Maybe running away is exactly what Merry was trying to do, and someone didn't let her."

Another of those long stares. "You have a name, mister?"

"John Slocum."

Bates nodded. "Thought so."

"Oh shit."

"You sure play hell on soap peddlers."

"Yeah."

"So why all this interest in the girl?"

"Kind of hard to say."

"Then that would make two of us, unless..." Something was changing in Bates' rugged face. Slocum realized it was a smile. "I was wondering where she got the stage fare," Bates said. "You know anything about that?"

"I might," Slocum said shortly.

"Was it voluntary?"

Slocum pretended to frown, as if he were puzzled. "Of course," he said. "She said she needed a stake to get out of here, and I happened to have a little extra."

"So you gave it to her, just like that."

Slocum tried to put Bates on the defensive. "Wouldn't you?"

The other man only shrugged, slowly. "If I had it." He lifted a spoonful of stew to his wide mouth, apparently lost in thought.

"Yeah, she did buy the ticket," he said after a while. "So it wasn't some kind of a house game. Was that what was bothering you? Anyway, I can tell you she never even showed up to get her money back."

"That's what's bothering me, friend. Tell me what you know about Al Swearingen."

"He's probably about as low as a man can sink, I'd say. But he's got plenty of friends and a lot of pull. He's dangerous. You better make particular note of that point, mister. The man's a scorpion."

It occurred to Slocum that he kept getting warnings about dangerous men. Not that it was any surprise. The wild opportunities of a gold rush would always bring out the scorpions.

"Was Merry scared when she bought her ticket?" he asked.

"I think so. Tried hard to hide it."

"Why didn't she wait for the stage right there?"

"I suggested it. She stayed for a few minutes, but then she said she had to fix something."

"Fix something? You're sure she didn't say someone?"

"Nope. She said something wasn't right and she had to take care of it. Said she'd be right back."

"She never said anything else?"

"Nope. Well, except for before. She asked me a couple questions when she was buying her ticket."

"What questions?"

"Well, names. She asked me if I'd ever heard of some jasper from Philadelphia. And then she asked me about you."

"What was the other man's name?"

"I don't recall. I'd never heard it before. But I told her all about you and that character with the soap." Bates leaned forward. "Tell me, is it true you kicked him in the balls?"

Slocum winced. "I broke his arm, for chrissake. Is that what you told her?"

"Not that part. I told her the rest, though, and maybe I shouldn't have."

"Why not?"

"Now that I'm thinking about it, that might have been when she started getting upset. It was just a few minutes later that she left."

Slocum wondered about her unfinished business. He found he was harboring a faint hope. He put it out of his mind.

"You ever see her again?" he asked.

Bates slowly shook his head.

"I appreciate your time," Slocum said, and he laid eight bits on the worn blue tablecloth next to the ticket seller's half-empty bowl. "I believe a hot steak will taste better than cold stew."

"Appreciated," said Bates.

"One more thing. Would there be any way of knowing what other property Swearingen owns in Deadwood?"

"You mean, where else could he hide Miss Atwood?"

Slocum nodded.

Bates seemed to think about it. "I've never seen the man anywhere else," he said. "As far as I know he lives right there."

Slocum stood up.

"By the way," Bates said quietly.

Slocum turned. After a moment he said, "Yes?"

Bates waited a moment, as if to make sure he had Slocum's full attention. "Hear me good," he finally said. "I told you all this because I don't think you have anything against the girl. But you oughta know. If you hurt her you'll regret it."

"I've already told you—"

"Yeah, you told me. But I got eyes, mister, and *they* tell me you're not going up against Al Swearingen just for the sake of Merry Atwood. You're not the type. Someone either hired you, or maybe she did take that money off you after all."

"I guess that's between me and her," Slocum said coldly. "And if I were you I wouldn't push my luck."

The two men stared at each other and neither one backed off. Bates spoke once more, in a quiet rock-solid tone. "That's all I had to say, Slocum. But I meant it."

10

From the dining room of the IXT Slocum needed only to climb
the stairs to find his room, which was in the same hotel. He
had decided to hang onto it even though he had yet to sleep
there. Now that he'd heard Bates's story—now that he was
deciding what had to be done—he was realizing there wasn't
much chance he'd sleep in it tonight either. But at least the
hotel would be a convenient place to get a bath and a shave
and to prepare for the night to come. The IXT was also considered the best lodging in the gulch. Not that that was saying
much. The railroad was still two hundred miles away, whether
you went south to Cheyenne or east to Pierre, so everything
brought into the Black Hills had to be hauled those two hundred
miles across the plains in cattle-drawn freight wagons. A poor
grade of green carpet covered the hall floor, and the paper on
the walls was already well worn.

Slocum stopped just inside the door of his room and scratched
a lucifer, nodding with satisfaction when the first flare of fire
showed his room in the same condition he had left it in two
nights before. While it still burned he used the same lucifer to
light a coal oil lamp on a small table, the smell of sulfur mixing
with the greasy smell of oil. Then he carried the lamp around
the room, tossing his bedroll on a chair and opening his warbag
on the bed.

Slocum's first order of business was to get that shave and
bath, followed by dinner downstairs. Warren Bates was gone,
and Slocum ate alone. He enjoyed a cheroot before he returned
to his room, but when he got there he went immediately from
the door to his warbag with a grim, fixed intensity showing in
his face.

Slocum dug out the second of his Colt Navies and a deerskin bundle and carried them to the small table by the door. He added the revolver from his holster to the collection and unfolded the bundle in the glow of the kerosene lantern. His moves now were obviously governed by long habit, but they were also precise and careful. Like any craftsman, Slocum knew that results depended on tools as well as skill. And for Slocum the desired result was staying alive.

The first thing from the deerskin bag was a Remington double derringer, placed on a corner of the table as a precaution in case he was interrupted. It could fire two .41-caliber bullets that would knock a big man flat on his ass. Now Slocum picked up each Navy in turn and pried loose the percussion cap from each chamber, discarding the caps. He then dug out the lead balls and gouged the black powder from each chamber in the cylinder, cleaning them thoroughly before holding the cylinder up to the light for inspection. He also inspected each bullet, discarding one that had been nicked, another that seemed poorly formed. He disassembled the guns themselves. He wiped each piece and oiled the moving parts, using a small can from the deerskin pouch. And all the time that he worked, another part of his mind was free to consider his problem.

Slocum decided to begin by assuming that Merry Atwood had told the truth about her arrival at the Gem Theater, or at the very least her desire to escape. It was always possible that she and Swearingen worked together to take money from the customers who seemed to have too much for their own good, but a scheme like that would put too much of a burden on the Gem's reputation. You could run crooked games and serve "trade" whiskey spiked with gunpowder and still be tolerated in a boom-town, but it would be going too far to rob your customers by the use of force. Pretty soon people would start going elsewhere.

The fact that Merry had actually bought a ticket also seemed to eliminate Swearingen as an accomplice. It had occurred to Slocum that the ticket seller himself was the one who had warned Swearingen that the girl was trying to get away, but Bates didn't seem the type. Bates also had that story about the last thing he had heard the girl say, and it didn't sound like the kind of thing a man would make up.

Slocum paused as he was reassembling one of the Navies and stared at the wall. What could Merry have been trying to "fix?" What would be so important that she would leave the safety of the stage station, so close to escaping her life in Deadwood? Slocum tried to picture her coming back to free him and to return the wallet that by then she knew belonged to the dead man. It was what he wanted to believe, but he had been disappointed too many times. He tried to think of other possibilities. None came immediately to mind. Slocum shook his head, baffled, pulling the hammer back on each gun and letting it down easy. Satisfied that they were working smoothly, he dug an old tin powderhorn out of his pouch and carefully began measuring new charges of black powder into the chambers. On top of each charge he laid a new wad and one of the lead balls, levering the rod below the barrel of the gun to pack all six chambers of each cylinder.

Slocum was still wondering where Merry Atwood might have gone when she left the station. It might help him figure out where she was right now. In his mind he saw her leaving the station with a ticket for the Cheyenne stage—the last thing he knew of her for a fact. From there he decided there were two possibilities. The first was that she had bought the ticket merely to lay a false trail. Slocum figured she was smart enough to do it, and she sure as hell had enough money. But he came right back to her comment about fixing something, and it didn't sound like something she would make up either.

Slocum was about as sure as he could be that Merry Atwood had planned to use her ticket. So why didn't she?

She either thought of a better idea when she went to take care of her problem—whatever it was—or Al Swearingen had caught up with her before she could go back to catch the stage.

Slocum carefully returned his cleaning tools to their pouch. The pouch itself he slipped into a coat pocket, out of habit.

If Merry was still free, she was either somewhere among the five thousand people crowding the gulch or well on her way home by some other route. If so, he'd never see his money again, and James Q. Eastman's fiancée would be a lot poorer in this harsh world. But Swearingen had claimed he knew of the girl's departure from the Gem—that he was on his way to find Slocum for that reason. So it seemed far more likely that

Merry had been caught. Which meant that Al Swearingen had Slocum's money—and had it, knowing who it belonged to, even while he was sending Slocum off on his fool's errand to stop the stage.

Slocum had a sleeve holster for the derringer. He put it on. One of the Navies went into his cross-draw holster, the other into the left pocket of his coat.

He stopped at the front desk on the way out, because the clerk looked like the kind of man who'd give straight answers.

"What have you got in the way of law?" he asked.

"Well now," said the clerk, a gleam in his eye, "technically this here's still an Indian reservation. No sheriff, 'cause we ain't got no county to put him in. No U.S. marshals, 'cause the first thing they'd have to do would be arrest us all for being here." The clerk took a closer look at Slocum. "We do got a town marshal, mister. But he ain't worth much."

"Good," said Slocum. "And thanks."

11

Slocum pushed through the door of the Gem Theater about an hour later, and his first impression was that he might have just stepped out for a minute or so and not for two days. The piano player played the same tunes, and the same girls were on the dance floor with the same sort of men. The air was filled with the same smoke, filtering the ever-present light from the smoky coal oil lamps.

This time, however, Slocum noticed Butcher as soon as he came through the door. Their eyes met and Slocum nodded. Butcher only stared back, his black eyes gleaming beneath a huge shelf of forehead and a heavy ridge of eyebrow. Slocum went to the bar and ordered a glass of the bonded whiskey. When he turned around Butcher had disappeared.

Slocum smiled.

He had made arrangements for the continued boarding of his packhorse, then brought his saddle horse to a different livery barn, this one at the edge of town on Whitewood Creek. The horse was waiting in one of the rear stalls. The back door of the barn was unlocked. The horse was well fed and fully rigged. Slocum's bedroll was tied behind the saddle, his warbag knotted to a thong on one side and his Henry securely in a scabbard on the other. The liveryman who had unlocked the back door would also make sure no one touched Slocum's outfit. The liveryman was a little richer than he had been an hour before.

It took no more than two minutes before Slocum saw the movement of a dark curtain along the back wall. He marked it as the entrance to Swearingen's office, but it was impossible to tell whether the curtain covered another hallway, or what kind of door protected the owner of the Gem from the unruly masses. There might even be more than one door.

Swearingen himself came through the curtain and threaded his way through the mob directly toward Slocum, followed by the brooding Butcher. Swearingen looked as happy as Butcher looked gloomy.

"How nice to see you again, Mr. Slocum!" said Swearingen. "I hope you have good news for me."

Slocum saw that Swearingen was carefully observing him as they talked, but only because Slocum knew what to expect. Merry had been right, he thought. This was one smooth article. "I'm afraid the news is all bad," he said aloud. "I missed the stage completely."

"Missed the stage," Swearingen repeated. "That is indeed a shame, sir. I'm sorry for both our sakes."

"I bet Slocum is sorry too," murmured Butcher.

"That will be enough," Swearingen said mildly.

"What did you do, Slocum, stop for a nap on the way?"

"Butcher!" A fierce edge had come into Swearingen's voice, and Slocum knew he was seeing the man's dangerous side. "I'm afraid Butcher is even more disappointed than I," said the owner of the Gem, sounding apologetic before the edge returned to his tone. "Perhaps it's because he feels partly responsible for my loss."

Slocum met Butcher's stare with a harsh one of his own. "I suppose in a place like this," he said evenly, "you have to hire any kind of lowlife you can find."

A long moment passed before Slocum spoke again, this time to Swearingen. "My horse threw a shoe on the rocks. Couldn't chance it."

"Perfectly understandable," said Swearingen, still watching Slocum's expression. "In fact, it may be that you avoided some unpleasant confusion, Mr. Slocum. The wire tells us that another man actually did stop the stage."

"I'll be damned," said Slocum, in a tone that was tinged with irony. "Someone else had the same idea?"

It was not Slocum's intention to fool Al Swearingen—only to make Swearingen think he was trying to fool him. He was trying not to act dumb, but to act like someone trying not to act dumb. That seemed to be the best way to generate the uncertainty he wanted to create.

"Yes," said Swearingen. "One man all by himself. And not far from the shortcut of which I told you. Of course, the wire also says the man had brownish hair and a scar on his neck."

"Was anyone hurt?" Slocum asked.

"Fortunately, no. The bandit was arrested."

"By who?"

"Apparently the superintendent of the line, Mr. Slocum. He happened to be riding at a discreet distance behind the stage."

"I feel sorry for the poor sap he caught," said Slocum. "Do you suppose he'll hang?"

Swearingen moved his head very slightly. Perhaps a nod of approval. "I doubt it," he said. "The gentleman escaped."

"Good for him. Perhaps he'll move on to healthier climates."

"Let's hope he does," Swearingen said quietly, holding Slocum's eye, and then suddenly the saloonman turned jovial. "I still haven't made it up to you for the unfortunate night you spent in one of our rooms. Mr. Spence"—he raised his hand toward the bartender and then pointed at Slocum—"this man is to have the best liquor in the house, at my expense. And all the dances he desires."

"Yes, sir," said the bartender.

Swearingen gripped Slocum's arm. "If I don't see you again," he said meaningfully, "I hope you have a pleasant stay."

Slocum watched the plump little man walk away through the crowd, with an occasional nod or a few words for a familiar face. He saw no direct communication with Butcher, but that man soon moved back into his position near the door. Swearingen continued his rounds of the saloon, chatting briefly with the piano player before disappearing once again behind the dark curtain. He never looked back toward the bar.

Slocum asked for a beer and four or five dance tickets. The bartender laid them out on the scarred wood counter and hurried off toward a drunken miner hollering for service, leaving Slocum alone to contemplate the dance floor. He didn't touch the beer. When the song ended Slocum caught up one of the returning girls and gave her a ticket. She had large, deep-set dark eyes and long black hair, but Slocum had also noticed a faraway look in her eyes, as though she wasn't really in the Gem. When they were dancing Slocum quickly told her what he wanted.

"Did you know Merry Atwood?" he asked the girl.

He felt her small hand squeeze his. She pulled back to look at him, frightened. "Merry?" she said. "What do you want with her?"

"I have to find her. Have you seen her?"

"She left."

Slocum glanced over the girl's head and across the room. He saw Butcher watching him closely.

"Just like that?" Slocum said. "Can you girls leave here whenever you have a mind to?"

"I . . ." The girl closed her mouth. She stopped dancing and pulled away. "I'm sorry," she said. "I have to go." She went to the other side of the hall and stood watching the dancers.

Slocum had no better luck with a redhead or a short blond-haired girl. He didn't really expect to. He saw Butcher watching every move. Slocum picked out another dark-haired girl who looked a little older than the others, and a hell of a lot harder. But he tried anyway.

"You mean you're only dancing with me because you want to find someone else?" she said. "I hope you weren't trying to make me feel good, mister, because it sure as hell isn't working."

Slocum laughed, because the girl was not entirely serious. "You're right," he said. "I forgot my manners. I should be horsewhipped for insulting a beautiful and intelligent woman."

"Now don't dab it on too thick, honey, or I won't believe a thing you say. But come to think of it, I'm tired of listening to men talk. Especially men who look like you. Were we going to do anything else besides talk?"

Slocum looked for Butcher again, and found him in a darkened corner talking to the first girl Slocum had danced with. Their heads turned toward Slocum, then quickly away. They kept talking, apparently so that no one else could hear them, and the girl with the big eyes was still looking frightened. He saw her shake her head once, and again, emphatically.

"Well?" said the dark-haired girl.

"As a matter of fact," said Slocum, "I think you've hit on a fine idea. Unfortunately, I may be in a bit of a hurry."

She took his hand. "You and me both, brother. Let's go."

12

Again Slocum was led by the hand through the door in the back wall, into the same dim hall lined with other doors. He heard the same noises behind them. But the dark-haired girl who led him this time paced down the hall like an excited bobcat. Slocum almost expected her to growl. She pulled him into one of the small rooms and faced him, already pulling her clothes off. She was shifting her weight from one foot to the other as if her hunger was so overwhelming that she couldn't keep still.

"Take off your damn pants," she whispered hoarsely. "I can't wait forever." She shifted her weight again and moved her hips from one side to the other. "Come *on!*"

Slocum was fumbling with his own clothes, infected by the girl's hunger and by the sight of her body in the candlelight. Her chest rose and fell with its labored breathing, swelling her breasts and thrusting them toward Slocum. He cupped them in his hands and kissed them, taking the hard nipples in his mouth while she stroked his hair and then reached down between his legs.

"Oh God!" she said. "Hurry up and put this where it will do some good."

Slocum still had his shirt on, the cuffs buttoned at the wrist because it was the last thing that hid the holster for the little Remington derringer. He started to tumble her onto the bed with him but she resisted, squeezing the hard muscle in his arms.

"The shirt too," she demanded. "I get so damn tired of all the potbellies and the drunks." She licked her lips and gave Slocum a mischievous grin before letting her eyes take in the full length of his body. "You are a wonderful sight for these old eyes, mister, and I want to see it *all.*"

Slocum took her in his arms and unbuttoned his cuffs behind her. He also unstrapped the holster and palmed the little gun it held. He had a quick mental picture of Butcher, in the saloon, questioning the other two girls Slocum had danced with. Perhaps he was already on the way to Swearingen's office with what he had learned.

The girl took the length of him in her restless hands and was bending it down to rub in the smoky hair between her legs. He could feel the dampness there, and then the contact with soft wet folds of skin. He shuddered and kissed her neck, shrugging out of his shirt. She helped strip it off and ran her palms along his arms and up over his powerful shoulders.

"I want to be on top," she whispered. "I want to be able to look at you and have you as deep inside me as you can go."

Slocum lay down on the rough straw mattress and the girl follwed him down, leaning on one hand and guiding him into her with the other. She closed her eyes and squirmed as she sat on him, moving her hips as though she couldn't get enough.

Slocum closed his own eyes, but he was imagining a discussion in Al Swearingen's office. He saw Swearingen frowning in concentration as he tried to understand Slocum's actions in the Gem Theater and tried to reach some kind of decision. Slocum also listened for sounds in the hall. He still held the derringer in his right hand, dangling over the side of the bed.

The girl was moving in a soft, steady rhythm, and Slocum watched her breasts swaying just above his face. They were beautifully rounded and firm. The girl opened her eyes and saw him looking, and smiled. "Squeeze them!" she said. "Grab them hard." The words seemed to excite her, and the rhythm quickened. Slocum wanted desperately to abandon the gun in his hand, just to lay it on the floor for a moment. But he'd been in the West too long to make that kind of mistake. He contented himself with laying that arm along her thigh and curling his clenched hand around the small of her back. He rubbed her breasts hungrily with the other hand, squeezing them in turn, rolling the nipples between his fingers.

The girl moaned and clenched her hips around Slocum's

cock. "Don't stop!" she pleaded. "Harder!" Slocum squeezed harder and she responded instantly, rocking back and forth on him, plunging him deep inside and then almost losing him, working herself into the kind of frenzy he'd seldom seen among the upstairs girls. But above her moans and rasping breath he heard the muted sound of a tight door hinge in the hallway. He held his breath, no longer aware of his hand on the girl's breast. He heard no steps—which a normal customer would certainly make—but he heard one squeak of a floorboard. Slocum cocked the derringer, sure that the girl heard nothing in her passion. Her hands were moving through the coils of thick black hair on Slocum's chest, and her contorted face shone with sweat. Suddenly Slocum felt her tighten around him, the grip of powerful muscles, and she was crying out with a final shiver that rippled down her body.

Slocum wasn't watching. His eyes were on the door, and he saw it swing open, Butcher coming in fast right behind it with that seven-inch knife held high in his hand. Slocum raised his own arm and let Butcher look down the two .41-caliber barrels. Slocum wished the gun itself was larger, but he figured the two wide-open bores would be enough to stop the killer. For a second it looked like he was wrong. Slocum's finger was just starting to squeeze the trigger when Butcher controlled his momentum, freezing in mid-stride.

The girl was still crying out, her eyes squeezed closed, and only now did she slump forward, moving against Slocum a few more times before sighing deeply and opening her eyes. They went round in fear.

Slocum grinned up at Butcher. "Even an asshole like you ought to know it's bad manners to interrupt a lady," he said.

The big man's black eyes were shining with hatred. Slocum ignored the look.

"And besides," he said with a grin, "I ain't ready just yet." Slocum had suddenly been aware of himself throbbing inside the girl, and now he felt his hips moving as if by themselves. It was a crazy idea, he thought, but there was a hunger there that wouldn't go away. The demanding ache in his loins would make it hard to concentrate on anything else.

"Drop that knife," he told Butcher. "Kick it under the bed

and press your nose in that corner, you son of a bitch. If I see so much as a twitch you're gonna have a couple of big holes in your belly."

With Butcher in the corner and Slocum trying to ignore the smirk on the man's face—he'd take care of that later—Slocum gave in to that pure physical demand and began bucking himself up into the girl swaying above him. The frightened look in her eyes had given way to a kind of private, satisfied smile. Perhaps she felt this was a sign of the power she had over men. She helped Slocum along with her hands, and he was rewarded almost instantly. The sensations burned through his blood and rushed along his skin. "Oh Lord!" he murmured, and the girl laughed softly.

"One good turn deserves another," she said, and bent slowly forward on her knees to let Slocum ease out of her. She kissed him playfully on the cheek, then nodded toward the hulking man in the corner. "What about him? I have to work for these fellows, you know."

The girl jumped off the bed to scoop up her dress. Butcher turned around, and Slocum kept his eyes on him as he spoke. "If he's got half the brains of a mule," Slocum said, "and I hope I'm not giving him too much credit, then he'll know I set him up. He'll know you didn't have anything to do with it."

"What do you mean, set me up?" snarled Butcher.

"I wanted you alone. And you're not gonna be too thrilled with what happens."

"We'll see about that."

Slocum eased into a sitting position and reached for his Colt in the tangle of clothes on the floor, replacing the derringer while he tried to dress himself with the other hand. The dark-haired girl helped him pull his clothes on once she had taken care of herself.

"You'd better go," Slocum said. "Tell Swearingen to pay you well and give you a big tip."

"I'm not sure who should pay who, sugar. But anytime you come back, ask for Roberta. Hear me? And in the meantime..." She reached inside Slocum's pants before he closed them. "In the meantime, you take care of this for me."

A kind of snarl came from the corner, and Butcher said, "If you know what's good for you, bitch, you better tell the boss what's going on."

The dark-haired girl looked at Slocum.

"Go ahead," he said. "Don't get yourself in any trouble. And don't worry about me."

But when the girl had closed the door behind her Slocum shook his head. "You just made it a lot harder on yourself, Butcher." He was already flipping the Colt around for a reverse grip, so that it added weight to his fist, and before Butcher could react Slocum drove the fist deep into his stomach.

13

"Where is the girl, Butcher?"

Butcher was doubled over, holding himself around the middle and gasping for air. Slocum landed a blow to his temple that laid him on the floor.

"Where is the girl?"

"What girl?" Butcher gasped.

Slocum kicked him in the side. "Tell me. Now!"

"Fuck you."

Slocum kicked him again, feeling the crunch of a rib even through his boot. Butcher winced, but he repeated himself. "Fuck you, Slocum."

Another kick, and the same words, and still another kick. "Talk, Butcher. I ain't got all night."

"That's right, Slocum. Swearingen's gonna kill you."

"Like you did?"

"You're luck's gonna run out, Slocum." He groaned and clenched his teeth. "I just hope it's me that has the pleasure."

Slocum pulled back his foot to strike again, but he stopped himself. He did not enjoy causing pain—or at least he didn't once his anger died down, even when someone had tried to kill him. But more important was the plan he had in the back of his mind. He'd already accomplished what he set out to do so far, and for the rest of the plan to work, Butcher would have to be reasonably able to get around. And even while he was thinking it out Slocum heard the connecting door to the saloon burst open. He heard a sudden surge in the volume of the music, which caused him to frown, and then came the pounding of feet in the hallway. Slocum leaped to the window and flung it open.

"Go ahead and run," Butcher croaked, struggling to rise. "You're a dead man tonight."

Slocum put one leg over the sill and fired a shot back through the bedroom door to make his pursuers think twice about coming through. The ball also passed within a few inches of Butcher's head. "Keep dreaming," Slocum said, and pushed himself through the window.

Slocum rolled when he hit, and kept rolling. He heard the crash of gunfire he was expecting, and he felt the ground shudder with the impact of slugs where his body had been an instant before. He also tried to place the muzzle flashes while he was rolling. He saw them in the window he'd just left, and in the deep shadows against the back of the building. Slocum had expected that too: a backup man to cover the escape route. He came out of his roll and into a crouch to snap off a shot at the window. First take care of the one who could duck away. He was jumping to the left almost as he fired, and the immediate barrage from the back of the building almost covered the scream of the man at the window. Beneath both sounds he heard the *thunk-thunk* of heavy bullets in the log wall behind him. With an instinct faster than thought, Slocum realized the man in the shadows was trying to bracket the muzzle blast from his own Navy, and Slocum sprawled to the ground perhaps even before he heard the bullets hit. With the same sure instinct he knew that a fighter smart enough to bracket his shots would already be on the move as well. And instead of conserving his rounds, as he had planned, Slocum instantly changed his strategy and emptied his Navy into the shadows—twice over to the left, once to the right, and one down. By now his ears rang with the explosions and the small alley had filled with smoke. If Slocum could hear nothing, he could see even less. It was time to be moving again. He could only hope he'd put his enemies out of commission for the moment.

He'd already studied the shortest route during his preparation. It lay between two buildings that backed the alley from a side street, and also shielded the alley from a direct view. Pedestrians on the side street wouldn't be able to tell where all the shooting was coming from, and if anything they would rush down to Main Street, where most of the traffic was. When

Slocum stepped calmly from between the two buildings he was not met with any particular attention. He had dropped the empty Colt into his coat pocket and put its twin in his holster. He joined the crowds milling on the boardwalk, and when the occasional passerby would say, "Where's all the commotion?" Slocum would shrug with a blank look and say, "Beats me!"

Slocum made his way back to Main Street, threading through the excited early-evening crowds and finding himself anonymous there, just as he'd expected. Within moments he had taken a place on a boardwalk opposite the Gem Theater, joining six or seven onlookers slouching beneath a small hanging sign that advertised the general merchandise for sale at "Joseph & Associates, Fine Retailers of Deadwood."

"What's all the excitement?" he asked the nearest man.

"Don' know, partner. A lotta shootin'."

Slocum stayed back in the shadows, behind the men who were content to remain on the boardwalk and wait for developments. There was another group like it around the open door of the Gem, the drinkers and dancers who'd rushed out to see what the shooting was all about. Only a few men had actually ventured into the dark little alley to the right of the building, where the thick blue haze of powder smoke was still drifting out into the street. Not long after Slocum arrived he saw a man emerge from the haze like a ghost and strut into the street with a great sense of his own self-importance.

"Man's been shot," he hollered. "Get the marshal."

"What about a doctor?" someone said.

The man shook his head. "No need for that."

Slocum nodded slightly and began watching the front door of the Gem. Several men edged out, curiosity seekers who worked their way up to the alley and glanced in, asking everyone around them what had happened. Slocum ignored them. The rest of the crowd at the door slowly drifted back inside, and in another minute Slocum heard the piano start up. That's when he also saw what he was waiting for—a thick-shouldered man moving stiffly and holding one arm to his side. Butcher. He was leading three other men. Two of them carried rifles. The other one and Butcher carried shotguns. Slocum saw them put their heads together, standing in front of the Gem. No one seemed to pay any attention. Butcher pointed down Main Street and one of the men broke away in a trot. Another headed in the opposite direction. Slocum saw Butcher point directly at him, or so it seemed. Butcher gestured to the final gunman, probably talking about the narrow streets of Forest Hill behind him, then the two of them split up and faded into the narrow back roads to the north and south of Main Street.

Slocum grinned, sucking in a tight breath that hissed through his clenched teeth. He waited one minute. Then he pushed himself away from the wall and ambled toward the front door of the Gem.

He was thinking about that surge in the volume of music when the hall door had burst open.

And how quiet it had been, on the other hand, when Butcher was sneaking toward the bedroom with the knife in his hand.

14

Slocum paused just inside the door, taking in the room with his eyes while he let them adjust to the dim glow of the coal oil lamps. The air was stale with hanging smoke and the smell of sweat. It no longer seemed to be the gay place he had thought it was. The music and the laughter were there just the same, but now they were only noise and Slocum was looking only for hostile faces. As far as he could tell no one was paying attention to him when he began his long careful walk toward the dark curtain hanging on the back wall.

He was maybe halfway there, congratulating himself for flushing Swearingen's gunmen out of the saloon, when he noticed the bartender edging toward the far end of his bar. The man was just beginning to reach down for something hidden under the counter when Slocum roared over the noise in the room.

"No!" he bellowed, freezing the bartender in surprise. Slocum had whipped out his Navy and unlimbered the derringer as well, one in each hand and pointing in generally opposite directions. He chanced a quick look around because the bartender was still frozen in a half crouch, staring at Slocum's Navy, and the men between them were scattering to either side. The noise was dying and the piano had quit and Slocum was almost able to whisper. "Whatever you got down there," he told the bartender, "you'd better treat it like a snake. Because you got my word it'll bite you."

The bartender put his hands on the counter in front of him. Slocum tried another quick look around. He caught sight of the tall and gutsy dark-haired girl. She gave him a wink. There was a total silence in the room now, not even the murmur of curiosity. Slocum saw only a mass of nervous and watchful faces. The move was his.

He started for the back curtain again, trying to watch everything at once, when he saw the curtain itself being lifted by a set of pudgy little fingers that had to be Swearingen's. The owner of the Gem showed his face for only an instant, long enough to find out why his saloon had suddenly fallen silent, and then the curtain dropped and he disappeared.

Slocum charged, scattering the would-be dancers as he ran. He flattened himself against the back wall and pulled at the curtain from the side, but there were no shots. He chanced a look and saw a hallway, almost pitch black, with only one door at the end. He ran at it and tried to smash it with his shoulder, careening off to flatten himself once again against a wall. This time there were two explosions. Holes appeared in the door, and splinters of wood stung Slocum's cheek. He heard a cry from the main room behind him. He cursed and landed a powerful kick near the heavy brass knob, again falling back against the wall, but the door held fast as if it were heavily reinforced. And this time there were no shots.

Slocum squinted his eyes and nodded absently, running back through the curtain. He was vaguely aware of someone on the floor, of a pool of blood and people kneeling down to try to stop the flow. But he was intent on the other hallway, the one that ran parallel to the first but led to the poor little cribs behind the dance floor. He had his hand on the entrance door when he heard a single gunshot behind him. From the way the concussion felt he didn't think the bullet was coming his way, but he automatically tensed for the blow. He whirled around to see the bartender leaning heavily against the counter, one hand over his shoulder and blood trickling through the fingers. The bartender looked down at himself and then frowned at Slocum, perplexed, as though he didn't quite understand what had happened or how in hell Slocum had done it.

Slocum was just as puzzled. He paused one more instant to scan the scores of anonymous faces watching the scene. He saw the dark-haired girl again—the one called Roberta—and cocked his head at her, but she only shrugged to say she didn't know anything either. Slocum had given up and was turning the doorknob in his hand when he did see one more familiar face. It belonged to Warren Bates, the stage line's ticket agent. He was back off in a corner, and Slocum noticed that a couple of the men in front of him were still looking at Bates. But the ticket seller was watching Slocum, almost no expression on his big square face, although Slocum thought that in the dull glow of light he could make out the trace of a smile, a kind of humor in the eyes. Slocum nodded at him once, got no reaction, and figured he'd spent enough time standing around.

He threw open the door to find Swearingen reappearing almost like magic, backing out of another door that opened onto the hall at Slocum's left. Swearingen's surprise cost him a second of hesitation while he stared, mouth hanging open. Maybe he was realizing his disadvantage, with his gun arm on the side away from Slocum. He started trying to bring it up, spinning around to give himself room. He also saw the Navy in Slocum's steady fist and had second thoughts. But by the time he reversed his momentum and tried ducking back into the room he'd just left, Slocum was already on top of him. He grabbed the neck of Swearingen's coat with one hand and smashed his Navy against the man's gun arm with the other. Swearingen screeched with pain, dropping his revolver from the deadened arm, and Slocum gave him a shove into the room that sent him sprawling on the floor. Slocum picked up the fallen gun—a fairly new Smith and Wesson—and dropped it in his coat pocket with a short nod of approval. It would help make up for the Colt he'd emptied in the alley. The derringer that had been in the pocket he slipped back into its wrist holster. Then Slocum closed the door behind him, threw home the three steel-mounted deadbolts, and fell into the nearest overstuffed easy chair. It was covered with a print of bright yellow daisies.

Slocum sighed deeply, looking around at what seemed to be a sitting room. He grinned at Swearingen, still on the floor.

"Say, is it always this hard to get an invitation?" he said.

Swearingen saw he wasn't about to be shot, and now he sat up, straightening his lapels and craning his head in a comical way to readjust the fit of his wrinkled suit. Slocum noticed the cunning look in his eyes. The fat saloonman was already trying to think his way out.

"Who told you?" Swearingen whined. "That little bitch? I'll have her skinned alive."

"You mean about the back door?" Slocum asked. "I'd say if you were stupid enough to let your whores know about it, that's what you'd deserve."

Slocum stopped to let it sink in. It'd be safer for Roberta if Swearingen convinced himself.

"Anyway," Slocum said, "I figured it out with the help of Butcher."

"Butcher!"

"Yup. And you too, for that matter." Slocum dropped the casual tone and focused his anger on the plump little man trying to look dignified while he sat on the floor. "When you sent Butcher in there to kill me—"

"Now wait a minute—"

"When you sent Butcher to kill me," Slocum insisted, "you had him use that door you just came out of. You probably figured it would be quieter. But it wasn't quiet enough, and then I put two and two together when I realized I hadn't heard all the usual noise that comes in when the front door gets opened. The rest was easy."

Swearingen's eyes glittered. He was studying Slocum. "I'm going to get up now," he said.

"No you ain't."

Swearingen shrugged. "You think you're clever," he challenged, tilting his chin to indicate the room they were in. "But this looks very much like a trap to me. My men will be back in a few minutes."

"Sure. They'll probably have as much luck breaking down the door as I did."

"You fool! I'm talking about going out of here."

"Don't worry, I'll be right behind you." Slocum grinned at the clever way he'd said it until he realized the owner of the Gem was looking a bit satisfied on his own. Slocum cursed himself, understanding instantly that Swearingen knew he would not be killed.

"And if you're not around to help," Slocum said coldly, "well, I've been in worse spots."

"Undoubtedly. Quantrill never did worry much about the odds, did he?"

"What?"

Swearingen grinned at the surprised look on Slocum's face.

Slocum shook his head. "You have got nerve," he said. "I'll give you that. There aren't too many people who'd talk out loud about the war."

Swearingen sneered at him. "It's fine to be a big hero and rough up a helpless soap salesman, Slocum—"

"A man that was trying to kill me."

"—but such things also bring notoriety and gossip. Your name floats from tongue to tongue through the gulch, and other deeds are attached to it by men who've known the name before."

"Then you know I mean what I say," Slocum growled.

"Exactly!" Swearingen's eyes were round with a kind of innocence, and suddenly he smiled. "Mr. Slocum, do you really think I would send Butcher in there to kill you? To kill the man whose name is on everyone's lips? In the presence of a witness? I might add that she is our very best. Was she satisfactory?"

"You got that much right," Slocum said grudgingly. He knew he was falling prey to the smooth tongue of a charmer, and at the same time he found it hard to resist.

"Mr. Slocum, I only asked Butcher to bring you here—when you were ready—so that I might learn why you are making such a fuss about Merry Atwood."

"Because I want to find her."

"But I told you—"

"You told me bullshit. You sent..." Slocum almost made a fatal error. Identifying himself as the man who had stopped the stage would make him useless to the stage line. He'd lose the anonymity he needed to infiltrate the stock thieves. He'd also lose the two-thousand dollars and maybe get arrested to boot, if Horatio Brown was mad enough. "You sent me on a damn wild goose chase, and I'm just glad I had the sense to ask a few questions before I left town. There was no girl on that stage."

"You don't say!"

Slocum stared at the saloonman. And then he scowled. "Cut it out, Swearingen. I know your game. Everyone does. You lure these nice girls up here, and then you turn them out. You ruin their lives. Let them commit suicide. And then you punish them if they try to run away." Slocum stood up, towering over Swearingen. He'd talked himself into a fury, and now he held the muzzle of his Colt Navy four inches from the fat man's forehead. "By God," said Slocum, "I ought to kill you right here and get it over with. I'd probably be saving a lot of people a lot of misery."

Swearingen saw Slocum's chest rise and fall with its heavy breathing, and he saw the closeness of his own death in the chill of Slocum's green eyes. "All right," he whispered. "All right, I am responsible for some of that. But not Merry. I never saw her again. That's the truth."

Slocum didn't move. The Colt was steady, still four inches above the bridge of Swearingen's nose. "Let me look in your safe then."

"My what?"

"You heard me."

"Why? What do you expect to find?"

"Not a thing, if you're telling the truth."

The owner of the Gem frowned and looked down at the floor. Beads of sweat were forming above his eyebrows. "All right," he said. "She came back here. We found her. But she's in good hands now." Swearingen tried another smile, but it was feeble. "I can see I won't get away with lying to you, Mr. Slocum. So I won't. And I swear Merry Atwood is well taken care of."

"Sure," said Slocum. "Let's see the safe."

"But—"

Slocum pressed the barrel against Swearingen's forehead.

"All right! Anything you say, Mr. Slocum."

Slocum pulled the gun back, noticing the deep ring it left indented in the fat man's flesh. "Get up slow," he warned. He turned the owner of the Gem to face in the other direction and searched him thoroughly. He found a small knife in a specially sewn pocket inside the man's coat.

Swearingen offered another weak smile. "After all," he said, "I run a saloon."

Slocum continued the search and came across a second revolver tucked in the top of Swearingen's boot, covered by the cuff of his trousers. Slocum hefted the gun in his hand.

"Quite a beauty, isn't it?" said Swearingen. "The army model. It uses a metallic cartridge, forty-four center-fire. And look. It breaks open at the top there, so you can reload the whole cylinder at once." With his hand pointing closer and closer to the gun, Swearingen made a grab. Slocum slashed at his knuckles. The saloonman only shrugged. "Keep it if you like," he said. "It won a gold medal a couple of years ago in Austria."

"You're too kind," Slocum said sarcastically. He grabbed the back of Swearingen's coat and marched him through the room into a kind of alcove. It led through a couple of strategic twists and turns before it ended in an office, with no sign of Merry. The office held a scarred oak desk with a rolltop, a large clock, a couple of chairs, a gun rack that was empty— Slocum assumed it had held the armament now being carried in the search for him—and a large floor safe. In one wall was the heavy outside door with steel plate around the knob and three more steel bolts, any one of which looked like it could hold up against a charge of dynamite. Slocum saw the two bullet holes in the wood.

"You know," he said, "you shot one of your own customers."

"Christ!" said Swearingen. "One more mark against me."

"Don't worry," Slocum sneered. "Everyone knows you're a compassionate man. You care about your customers."

"It's your fault," stormed the fat man. "You should have left well enough alone."

"Why didn't you just sit tight in here yourself?"

"Because," Swearingen said sullenly, "I wanted to let the others know you had come back."

"But I thought you just wanted to talk to me to begin with."

Swearingen opened his mouth, but nothing came out. For once he seemed to be at a loss for words.

"Open the safe," said Slocum.

The owner of the Gem took another look at Slocum's eyes and bent over the safe. Slocum didn't see the dials turning but he heard them, and when he heard the final turn, followed by the click of the handle, he shoved Swearingen roughly aside and swung open the heavy door himself. A little pepperbox lay on one of the shelves, a gun with four barrels that could be fired all at once. Slocum looked at Swearingen, who was sprawled on the floor again, sucking one of his fingers, and showed him the pepperbox before it became the third gun in his coat pockets.

"My, my," he said. "You saloon owners must lead a terrible hard life."

Slocum returned his attention to the safe, and this time he saw the tan pigskin wallet he was looking for, entrusted to him by a man who'd been killed over some bars of soap, then stolen from him by a good girl from Ohio who had gotten trapped into being a whore. Slocum just stared at the wallet for a moment and shook his head, thinking: Life sure is a bundle of tricks.

He suspected another trick as soon as he picked up the wallet. It was a lot thinner and lighter than he remembered, and inside he found no identification. He also found only three hundred and five dollars, along with his two double eagles.

"Where's the rest?" he asked Swearingen.

"The rest of what?"

"Don't play dumb with—"

"Honest," said Swearingen. His eyes were round again, and he was holding up his hand. "That's exactly what she was carrying when we found her."

It occurred to Slocum that there was just an outside chance the saloonman was telling the truth. A chance of maybe one in a thousand, of course, but the point was that if it were the truth, then Merry must still have the money. And if Swearingen figured that out, he'd have good reason to make sure he got to her before Slocum did. He decided to go for the long odds, thinking the safety of the girl was more important than the money.

Slocum shrugged. "Then I guess that's all there was," he said. "I just don't know when I can believe you. Now tell me where the girl is."

Swearingen's face fell. "You don't really want her, do you? I assure you she's—"

"Yeah, I know, she's safe. She's all taken care of." Slocum raised the Colt again, the gaping barrel only an inch from

Swearingen's right eyeball, and slowly cocked the hammer. "Where's the goddamned girl?" he roared.

Beads of sweat were popping out on Swearingen's forehead. The man looked miserable. "I can't tell you," he said.

"What!"

"I sold her. It doesn't matter anyway, Slocum. You'd never get her back."

"I appreciate your concern. But I'll take my chances."

Swearingen was shaking his head in his misery. "I can't tell you who I—who she's with. He'd kill me."

"So will I."

Swearingen looked up, pleadingly. "I pray you won't, sir. But the fact is, I don't believe you will. You don't have the reputation of a cold-blooded killer."

"Damn my reputation."

Swearingen's eyes held steady on Slocum's. "I'll have to take my chances. There is no question with this other man. He *is* a cold-blooded killer, and I know I would be dead within a week."

"So you sold Merry to a cold-blooded killer."

"I was angry. I know it was terrible, but I—"

Slocum brought the barrel of the gun down on Swearingen's temple and kicked him hard in the gut. "By God," he said, "I'll beat you until you tell me." He kicked again, in a wild fury. He slashed down with the Colt. "I'll beat you until you're begging me to die."

Swearingen was shaking his head. "It's pointless," he said, his voice a pitiful wheeze. "You're wasting your time. I'm not a strong man, Slocum, but I can withstand great amounts of pain. And I'd rather be a cripple than a dead man."

Slocum kept pouring blows over Swearingen's back and face, but after a moment he knew the fat man had finally spoken the truth. The beating didn't seem to affect him as it should. And just then he heard the pounding of boots in the little hallway. Someone started banging on the door. There were similar sounds coming in through the sitting room.

"Boss!" said a voice. "Are you in there? Are you okay?"

"Open up!" shouted another voice. "This is the marshal."

Slocum glanced at Swearingen, ignoring the rest of the pounding and yelling. "The town marshal?" he asked.

Swearingen nodded, holding his midsection, apparently finding it painful to speak.

"Who's he answer to?" Slocum said.

"To us. The business people."

"He can't have any authority. Hell, we're not even in the United States. Technically speaking."

"He can set the other law on you," Swearingen gasped. "He can get a posse up."

There were more shouts, more fists pounding on the door.

"And of course the posse will include the Butcher and your other hired help," Slocum said bitterly. "Swearingen, the world will be a better place if you don't live another night. But right now I have to admit you're gonna be helpful."

Slocum motioned with his Colt and Swearingen got to his feet just as someone started firing blindly through the door.

"Damn it all," Swearingen said. "Rich Sandler has to be the craziest marshal any town has ever hired anywhere."

15

John Slocum edged sideways along the back wall of the Gem Saloon, Al Swearingen's fat neck locked in the crook of his arm. The top of the man's head just cleared Slocum's chin. Butcher and the three other gunmen watched intently from where they stood beside the town marshal and one of his deputies. All six men had piled their guns back in the hallway when Swearingen explained his situation through the locked door, hollering frantically at first to stop the shooting.

Now Slocum kept a tight grip on Swearingen's neck to discourage any thoughts of escape, and everyone in the room could hear Swearingen's labored breathing. They also saw the swollen bruises on his face, and the blood pouring from ugly gashes in his scalp. Slocum was getting a few hard looks from the people who were watching. He was glad for the Smith and Wesson he held in front of Swearingen, pointing down for the moment but ready just the same. The one loaded Colt was in his right hand, cocked and aimed at Butcher's bunch.

Slocum and Swearingen reached a corner and started shuffling down the side. Swearingen's blood was soaking Slocum's sleeve.

"How the hell do you expect to get out of town?" the marshal demanded. Rich Sandler had the sullen look of a badman himself, probably a law breaker in other parts of the country who fit in well with the gamblers, thieves, and con men running things in the gulch.

Slocum didn't answer. He just put the Colt to Swearingen's head.

"You can't cover your back forever, Slocum. Why not just give it up right now?"

"I have this idea I want to keep breathing."

"Shit, the only killing you done was self-defense. We'll just give you a ride out of town."

"You might," said Slocum. "But your friends here are aimin' to make sure it'll be my last ride on this earth."

"You can count on it," said Butcher. "I told you once, you're a dead man tonight."

"Now see what I mean, mister marshal? I'm not sure it's legal to go around killing people. Is it, mister marshal?"

Sandler scowled at Butcher and then looked generally disgusted. Slocum wasn't too happy either. He was rounding the last corner before the outside door and he felt ridiculous, like a crab he'd seen one of the times he was in California. The dark-haired girl was enjoying herself, though. Hers was the one friendly face in the crowd, and Slocum hoped Swearingen didn't notice the amused grin she wore. Thinking of friends, Slocum looked for Warren Bates. But the ticket seller had disappeared.

Leaving the saloon would be the tricky part. To keep Swearingen as a shield against the men inside, Slocum would have to expose his back to the street for a few seconds. He ordered the front door opened before he got there. He saw a couple of the waiting gunmen lick their lips, anticipating the chase and perhaps the kill. He edged to the open doorway. Through it he heard the plodding of hooves and the jangle of harness, the sounds of people laughing and the tune of a banjo from another saloon. Whatever might be waiting at least had not attracted a lot of attention. He ought to be able to handle it. He looked back at the gunmen and the marshal. They were poised to spring for their guns. It would take a few seconds to untangle the pile, but only a few.

"Now," said Slocum, talking over the top of Swearingen's head. "I've got a lot of dark streets and sizable crowds to get lost in out there. And then I'm plannin' a little trip for my health. If I stay lost, that is. Think about it. We could all be happy that way." Slocum used the Colt to point at Swearingen. "I'll leave this piece of shit in the doorway here. If I see anyone else, I'll kill him. And I'll kill you if you make one wrong move, Swearingen."

Slocum took a deep breath and whipped around the door frame, dragging Swearingen with him in a kind of snap-the-whip that didn't leave him exposed for very long. He took a quick look up and down the street and then started backing away. He left the saloonman blocking his own entrance, and kept his Colt leveled in Swearingen's direction. He glanced around again, just in time to see a rifle coming up in the hands of a shadowy figure which had been waiting under the same "Joseph & Associates" sign where Slocum had posted himself only a few minutes before.

Slocum didn't duck or flinch. He spun and aimed and fired his Colt so fast that it looked like a snap shot. Many men would not have been able to follow his movements. Slocum fired twice, and only then did he duck away. The man across the street took the slugs in his heart and lungs, but staggered back with his rifle still beside his cheek. With his heart blown to pieces, he still had the will to pull the trigger once. The ball smashed a pane of glass only a foot behind Slocum. Then the rifle clattered to the boardwalk and the man who'd held it staggered to the rail, supporting himself for a moment before he collapsed.

Slocum saw none of it. He was running down the center of Main Street, where it was darkest, dodging between horses and freight wagons and the unruly oxen which pulled them. Within a few yards he reached Wall Street—the deadline, beyond which the respectable businesses had long since closed for the night—and here he turned right, toward Deadwood Creek and the early beginnings of a Chinatown. From the corner he looked back toward the Gem and saw Butcher and his bunch filling the doorway. He was almost out of sight when he saw one of the gunmen look his way and raise his arm to point. He heard a shout, and saw the other faces turn—and then he was around the corner, cursing his luck. The only thing he had going for him were the deep shadows of dark streets.

The going got rough within a few yards, with more dips and turns and holes in the street as it got closer to the creek. The first placer diggings had torn up most of the gulch. The miners would dig down to bedrock, running the gravel through their sluice boxes, and pile the tailings somewhere else. It was all loose and slippery gravel, none of it level, shifting beneath Slocum's feet as he ran. He stumbled twice, trying to judge the lay of the land in very dim starlight. He sprinted into the creek channel, slipping into the water and running low, back in the direction of the Gem—and his stabled horse.

Slocum felt a little water slosh into his boots and he cursed again, marveling at the things a man could get himself into just because he tried to act a certain way. He needn't have given his word to send the pilgrim's money to his fiancée, but it seemed easy enough at the time, and it seemed like the right thing to do. Shit, he thought, I'd probably have done the same damn fool thing even if I'd known about all this. Stopping a stage, for chrissake! Then going in alone against a crooked saloon owner and his pack of hired guns. Slocum shook his head as he ran. It was nice having your word mean something. But no one ever said it would be easy.

Slocum had made it up to what he figured was Lee Street. He popped his head over the ditch bank and saw a couple of the gunmen, but they didn't see him. He turned sharply up the bank and around a little log hut, running for the hillside just a few feet away.

He was thinking about Merry Atwood. He was thinking that the money and the promise weren't the only reasons he was out here, trying to outrun a bunch of killers in the dark. It was also the promise he had made that a girl couldn't believe. The girl had begged him for help, and he'd been thinking of fortunes in gold. It wasn't that he had said no, it was just that he hadn't said yes good enough. After he'd thought about it—after he'd had a chance to calm down a bit—he figured it was partly his fault she'd taken a chance on the stage. Partly his fault that she'd gotten caught, and now she was being forced to fuck some murderer out in the woods.

Slocum shook his head again, this time to get hold of himself. He was working up the kind of anger that could lead him into making mistakes.

There were no trees on the hillside, just a forest of stumps looming in the starlight. When the first white men came into the gulch they'd found it choked with thousands of fallen and decaying trees, apparently the aftermath of some great disease or infestation. The awesome clutter gave the town of Deadwood its name. There had also been a young forest climbing the slopes in every direction. But the deadwood had warmed the first settlers through two winters now, and the nearest live trees had built their sluice boxes and their homes.

Slocum angled across a hump in the hillside, running behind some more rude log huts. He stumbled down into a dark ravine and up the other side, always looking over his shoulder, always looking for natural cover. Twice he thought he heard other men running behind him, but if they were they had given up. Slocum ran easily now, showing no strain. The years of work and hard riding had toughened him, and there was something in that knowledge that made him glad. He was running from a pack of killers, but he was grinning as he ran.

He came to another wash on the hillside, and from the ridge beyond it he knew he'd be able to see the livery stable that held his pony. It would be lying there just beyond the creek, where the Whitewood came churning in, and the back door would be only a dozen feet from the safety of the creek bed. Slocum ran up the side of the last ridge, moving well, slipping on loose rock now and then but adjusting instantly. He ran with the Colt in one hand and the Smith and Wesson in the other, stopping just short of the top to take a look at things below.

What he saw made him curse. He let the guns dangle at his side while he tried to understand it.

He saw a shadow leaning against the wall of the stable, a big man he couldn't identify. But while he watched, the shadow moved. Slocum squinted his eyes. He saw the stranger put a hand to his eyes and take a long look down the creek, then up to the ridge where Slocum was standing. Slocum had to resist the urge to duck. He knew that only a few inches of his head would be exposed above the heavy shadows of the ridge line. Now the stranger took his hand down and used it to point toward the stable, or so it seemed. And then the man shoved his hands in his pockets and leaned back against the barn again, leaving Slocum bewildered.

Had he been seen after all? If not, who was the shadowy stranger signaling to? Was he one of the hunters, signaling another one somewhere behind Slocum?

Slocum didn't move, except for a deliberately slow turn of his head that let him take in everything around him, pointing his ears in one direction and then another. He could see no other movement in the tricky light from the stars, and kept trying to make as little movement or noise as he could himself. He fell to watching the stranger again.

Twice more the man by the barn repeated his movements, and Slocum found himself thinking of the little clocks being brought over from Germany, with the tiny figures that come out every so often. Each time the man would lift his hand to shade his eyes from the stars while he looked downstream and then up toward the ridge. Twice more he made exaggerated pointing movements toward the barn, and then leaned back against the wall.

On the third go-round Slocum knew who it was. He recognized the tall hulking form and the slow, deliberate movements of Warren Bates. He also decided that the stage line employee hadn't seen him, after all—that he was *trying* to see something, and then pointing at the barn in an effort to pass on a message to whoever might be watching. Slocum couldn't figure out how Bates had gotten to be there, but he figured he was the one the message was for. He couldn't put anything else together that made sense, unless there just happened to be another fugitive running around out here tonight who also happened to be heading for this same barn.

Once he got that far, Slocum figured the message behind the pointing had to be a warning. And Slocum cursed again. He had to remember that not everyone took an oath as seriously as he did his. The liveryman had seemed reliable enough, but maybe when he heard the shooting he thought of ways to increase his fortunes for the night. Maybe he even thought he was being a law-abiding citizen. Maybe Swearingen's gunmen had come by while Slocum was palavering with the owner of the Gem, and the liveryman had gotten scared. Slocum had to admit this would be a tough town to live in.

However it had happened, Slocum decided, there could be only one meaning behind the message.

Someone was waiting for him inside.

16

Slocum took his time studying the layout of the buildings and noticing where the corrals were behind the barn. He found himself gazing at the lighted windows and the open campfires that twinkled beyond the town, up and down the gulch. He thought it would be nice to have a cup of coffee in his hand and a seat by a warm fire. All he felt was a chill in the air, and all he had to look forward to on this night was more shooting, and being shot at, followed by a lot of hard riding. And that was if he got lucky. Otherwise there'd be even more shooting to go along with the hard riding.

He looked again at the livery barn. The corrals fanned off to the right, between him and Warren Bates. Most of the horses inside were standing quietly. Slocum noticed a stack of hay bales outside the far corner of the corral. It was only a few paces from the hay to the back end of a store of some kind. From the ridge he could see the heavy timbers of the building, hewn square, and the planks of the false front rising above the roof.

Slocum thought he saw a flicker of movement by the creek, back where he'd gone across. But that was the only sign he saw of any pursuit. Which worried him. They may have split up when they lost sight of him, trying to search the whole town, but they also might have gotten smart. They might have posted themselves at key points around Deadwood, hidden in the shadows but watching the exits Slocum might use. They'd be almost impossible to spot until it was too late. But Slocum had no choices left, and by now he'd spent a quarter of an hour on the ridge without detecting any other activity—except for the steady, slow routine of Warren Bates.

Slocum backed off the ridge and slowly worked his way down the wash, his boots shuffling quietly in the dead pine needles and other debris collected there. He felt safer in the deep shadows of the little cleft in the mountain, and he'd also seen that it ended below the corrals, between the barn and the place where he had taken to the woods. He figured he could avoid being seen by anyone peeking through the back door of the barn, or by anyone who might be waiting for him in the other direction.

He loped down the creek channel a few yards, bent low, and came up over the bank behind the store he'd seen from the ridge. He'd guessed right. The bales of hay were between him and the stable barn. He ran to the store and flattened himself against the rough log surface, blending into the shadow. His hands against the wood came away with spots of sticky sap, and he could smell the mud that had been used for chinking. He heard no strange sounds above the distant thread of music from the saloons, and he saw no activity in the nearby streets or up on the hill. He crouched and made a run for the hay.

He studied the pile as he ran, and with a few swift movements he was able to hollow out a little opening in the stack. A few bales thrown up here, a few there, and he was out of sight from every direction but the empty store. He only prayed he had not been seen by someone stationed on the hillside.

Now he slipped around the edge of the stack until he could see the side of the livery barn and the dim figure of Warren Bates. Slocum carefully struck a lucifer cupped in his hands and held it beneath his chin for a moment before he blew out the flame. The light had blinded him, but he could hear—just barely—the whisper of approaching footsteps. Slocum slipped back to the protection of the hay bales and waited, Colt in hand.

The ticket seller came around the corner with his hands partly raised to show they were empty, and Slocum nodded with admiration. The man may have looked slow on the outside, but there was nothing slow about his thinking.

Bates glanced at the little hollow Slocum had made, and his teeth showed white in the starlight. "This your new home?"

"What's your recommendation?" Slocum murmured.

Bates squated on his haunches so he could whisper in even lower tones. "Well—"

"Wait a minute," said Slocum. "First the Gem. Was it an accident your being there tonight?"

"I go there off and on."

"Yeah, but tonight?"

"Well—" Slocum saw the ticket seller's teeth again. "I got to admit to a bit of curiosity, Slocum. After all, I missed your meeting with the soap man. So when you started asking about Merry and Al Swearingen . . . well, of course it was no accident."

"You shoot the bartender?"

"Yeah."

"Why?"

"He was about to do the same to you."

"I mean *why?*"

Bates seemed to shrug. "I guess I ain't so fond of Swearingen and his crowd. I also wanted to see what you were up to, and I figured you'd have to be alive to do it."

"Well, I'm obliged, Mr. Bates. Will it cause you trouble?"

"I don't think so. None I can't handle. Anyway, I'm the one obliged to you for making life unpleasant for Al Swearingen."

Slocum scowled. "Not unpleasant enough," he whispered. "The son of a bitch claims he sold Merry Atwood as punishment for trying to run away."

"To who?"

"Won't say. I don't think I could make him say. Not that I'll have much more of a chance on this night." Slocum felt he was being judged. "How'd you come to be here?" he asked.

"A feelin' I had," whispered Bates. "Butcher and the marshal come back with their men while you were still in having it out with Swearingen. But they didn't do anything right away. Not till after they talked with the bartender a bit."

"He hurt bad?"

"I didn't shoot to kill," Bates said shortly.

"What about the other man?"

"Swearingen killed *him*, by God. Got 'em right through the neck. Someone said he was a farmboy. From Vermont."

"Damn it. What'll the marshal do?"

"You mean after he gets done looting the boy's pockets?"

The two men were silent for a moment. Slocum could smell the sweet-sour hay, and he heard the rustle of Bates shifting his weight.

"Anyway," said Bates, "after the gabfest with the bartender I saw Butcher was giving orders. He was talkin' low so's no one could hear him, but he was pointing somewhere, and when he got done two of the marshal's men went out the door."

"You followed?"

Bates lifted his shoulders and let them fall. "Guess I'm just the curious type. One of the gents took up residence across the way, but I figured you could take care of him by yourself."

Bates paused, and Slocum answered with a nod.

"It was the other one that puzzled me. He kept goin' on up the street, like he knew just where to."

"Here?"

"Yup," said Bates. "He come right here. Talked with the liveryman a bit and then he went inside. Ain't come out since."

"Damn him!"

"Well now," whispered Bates. "I wouldn't be too hard on old Henry there. They probably told him how you'd killed a couple men. Not that they'd tell him why, of course. And I hate to say it, but he's still fool enough to think a marshal's badge means something. Even in a place like this."

"Too bad Henry couldn't've seen Butcher giving the orders."

"A lot of things Henry should see," Bates said bitterly.

Slocum frowned. "Just what is your complaint against Swearingen, anyway?"

Bates stared at the ground maybe almost half a minute before he answered. "A girl," he finally said.

"Not just any girl, I take it."

"You can say that again! She was—aw hell, Slocum, I'm talking about Merry."

"Merry Atwood?"

"Yeah." Bates was turning sullen, his voice a bit hoarse. "Damn it, you were with her. You know what I mean. She was . . . different from the others."

"She was that," Slocum agreed. Most whores didn't hit their customers over the head.

"I don't just mean she was a better . . . that she was good."

"You're in love with her, right?"

"I don't know. Maybe."

"I'm sorry, Bates." Slocum was thinking about Merry Atwood, wondering if maybe it was already too late. He was thinking that a woman with her spirit wouldn't give up right away, even if it was true she'd been sold to a killer. He also knew it might be wishful thinking.

He let the silence grow for a while, and suddenly heard a squeal of hinges. Bates automatically slapped his hand on the butt of his holstered gun. Slocum disappeared around the corner of the haystack, trying to get a look at the barn. He found he had to try the other side, ducking in behind the corrals, to get a view of the back wall. Just as he caught sight of it he saw the big barn door swinging closed.

Slocum tensed, listening for footfalls in the corral, but he heard nothing else. The horses stayed quiet. The more he thought about it, the more it seemed like the door had only swung a couple inches when it closed. Whoever was in there was probably just taking a look. He was getting impatient, and that was always a mistake.

"Just one man?" Slocum asked when he was back in his hiding place.

"Far as I know. But I imagine the shots will bring a lot more running."

Slocum nodded. "Look, Bates, maybe we can still find her."

"Find Merry? You think so?"

"Swearingen's the key, right?"

The ticket agent groaned. "When I think of what I'd like to do to that scum. He's the one that brought her out here."

"Did you ever try talking to Marshal Sandler?"

Bates let out a sound of disgust.

"Just asking," Slocum said mildly.

"He's Swearingen's man! The other businessmen too—and some of them aren't too crooked—but things pretty much go the way Swearingen wants 'em to, and he's the worst one of the whole damn bunch."

Slocum was excited. He leaned forward, and his voice was a hoarse sound. "Do any of those rumors say who he might associate with? I mean, does he have any criminal connections?"

"There's talk, Slocum. But so far I haven't heard any particular names."

Slocum sat back with a curse.

"Why?"

"The other thing Swearingen said in there—he told me he'd sold Merry, but he wouldn't tell me who because he was afraid. He said the man was a cold-blooded killer."

"The bastard!"

"I think we already agreed on that. I just wish I knew where to begin looking."

"Well," said Bates, "I told you there weren't any names to the rumors. But that doesn't mean I haven't come up with a few ideas my own self."

"Who?"

"Swearingen has a good game going, you know. His girls overhear things in the saloon, or some of the men get to bragging back in the cribs. Might be a miner who's made a killing and's getting ready to take his gold out. Or some road agent who thinks he's about to make a killing. So sometimes Swearingen comes by to give me a tip, see. A friendly hint that something might happen on such and such a run."

"An old story. As old as the first gold camp. A lot of poor slobs have sold themselves out never knowing."

"Whiskey and women," said Bates. "One hell of a combination." He seemed to think of something. "In fact, Swearingen told me there was going to be trouble the morning Merry bought the ticket. Know anything about that, Slocum?"

With a sigh, Slocum finally told him about his meeting with Merry Atwood. He felt like a fool. But he held fast to the story of a thrown shoe and a missed chance to stop the stage.

"Just as well," said Bates. "Our superintendent went along on that run, and he's a good man. There was an attempt on the stage after all, but the fellow got away."

"Maybe Swearingen sent two of us."

"It wouldn't surprise me."

"By the way, Bates, where was Merry headed?"

"Cheyenne."

"How much was the ticket?"

"Twenty-seven dollars. Why?"

"Just curious." Slocum wasn't looking at Bates, but he felt the ticket seller's inquisitive stare. "So," said Slocum. "Do you think Swearingen is working both sides? He tells you, and he tells the bandits?"

"Something like that," Bates said slowly. "I mean, it'll look good to the real law when we finally get some in here. He can try to pass himself off as lily white. But I've come to notice something in the past year, something kind of peculiar."

"What are you talking about."

"There's one particular bunch of bandits he never hears anything about. It's probably the worst bunch that operates in the hills, and I doubt they have any rules against patronizing the Gem Theater, but somehow Swearingen has never passed on any of their plans."

"Just the competition."

"Exactly!"

"And you're thinking if Swearingen's tipping them off—if he's friendly with the gang—"

"Merry would never be able to run away from them. She'd be stuck in the middle of nowhere."

"With a cold-blooded killer to tell her what to do."

"Seems pretty likely."

"Look," said Slocum. "Will you try and keep half an eye on things going on here? Where Swearingen is keeping himself and so on?"

"My pleasure."

"What am I looking for?"

"It'll be tough, Slocum. The gang is well organized, and they're ruthless, and no one knows where they operate from."

"What do you know?"

"The talk is that it's run by a fellow named Bill Chambers."

"I'll be damned," Slocum whispered.

"My boss has been trying to get something on him for months. Chambers has taken to calling himself Persimmon Bill, and they say he killed an Army sergeant in Wyoming. If you

can do anything about him while you're getting Merry back—
well, I'm sure the stage line would show it's gratitude somehow."

Slocum felt a wild urge to laugh, but he held it back. "I'll
be damned," he said again.

17

Warren Bates was the first to leave the protection of the hay bales. He argued about it, wanting to stay and help if necessary, but Slocum told him he'd already done enough without hurting his position in Deadwood. Slocum wanted to be able to sneak back into town, operating from Bates's home, but he could do that only if Bates and Slocum weren't connected. Bates agreed to the logic, and to giving Slocum refuge. He also promised Slocum he'd send a message to Horatio Brown, although he didn't fully understand it.

"Just tell him, 'Be on hand,' and sign it JS," said Slocum.

"Just the words and initials?" said Bates. "Nothing else?"

"Nope. Put it on paper and give it to one of the shotgun guards on the next run."

"Seems to me you're being pretty closemouthed, Slocum."

"Not my decision, Bates. Sorry."

The message was almost an afterthought, the result of Slocum's ability to evaluate everything he learned and keep it organized. The more he thought about the possible connection between Swearingen and the Chambers gang, the more he thought it unlikely that his original plan would work. If the ticket agent's guess was true, then it wouldn't be long before Swearingen learned of the new outlaw to join the gang—and Bill Chambers would hear about the man named Slocum who had mysteriously disappeared from Deadwood. It wouldn't take too much intelligence to make the connection.

"I might as well get started," Slocum said.

The stage man nodded and poked his head around the corner.

"Just go back casual," said Slocum. "Like you were out for a walk, maybe."

"I do that sometimes." Slocum heard a bit of resentment.

"And Bates," said Slocum, extending his hand. "I owe you."

The two men shook. Bates showed the faint white glow of teeth again. "Amazin' what I'll do for a man who buys me a steak," he said. Then he was gone.

Slocum gave him a full ten minutes, waiting quietly among the bales. He heard no shots or other disturbances. And by the end of ten minutes he was sure Bates wouldn't be connected with any disturbance at the livery barn.

The Colt Navy had never been out of Slocum's hand. Now he shifted it to his left and worked the fingers of his right hand a few seconds to get the stiffness out of them. From a crouch he also practiced a few left-handed moves with the gun, suddenly bringing it into play, aiming at a window pane, holding it from the hip. He felt a bit awkward, but it was good enough. He studied the street beyond the store one last time, studied the barren hillside and the meandering ditch of Deadwood Creek, then made his way toward the barn.

Slocum held himself to the side of the corral, hoping the horses wouldn't spook and taking that chance for the padded footing of hay and dirt that spilled over beneath the poles. He could barely hear his own sounds. From the corral to the back of the barn his senses were even sharper. He was within just a few feet of the man waiting for him on the other side of a thin board wall, and he was in plain sight of anyone who might be stationed up the hill. He waited for a shout, but it didn't come. He padded softly to the back door of the barn, the one he'd seen open up a crack and then close. He kept thinking: One false step, one broken twig, and a shitload of bullets could come tearing through those puny one-by-sixes.

But if he was lucky, there'd be no shooting at all.

Slocum waited just behind the door. He let the minutes stretch out. A half hour came and went, and still he waited. He knew that Butcher and three other killers were looking for him, along with the marshal and his men, and maybe some new recruits by now.

But Slocum waited, knowing the man inside the barn lacked patience. And knowing that, Slocum also knew he wouldn't have to go barging through a narrow door into a pitch-black barn, forcing the gunplay that would tell everyone where he was.

While he waited, Slocum thought about the tan pigskin wallet in his pocket, with three hundred and five dollars. In his mind, with not too much effort, he was able to add twenty-seven onto that. He came up with three hundred and thirty-two dollars. Somehow he wasn't surprised. Now he was working with nice round numbers. When Merry counted the money in the deadman's pocketbook, she had found exactly one thousand dollars more than that. So somewhere between the musky-smelling crib and Al Swearingen's safe, the scrip had disappeared.

Slocum was thinking about how many times the wallet had changed hands, wondering whose hand held the thousand dollars, when the barn door hinges made a small sound and a crack appeared almost in front of Slocum's nose. He saw four fingertips curl around the edge of the door, pale in the starlight. Slocum instantly grabbed for the hand behind the door, gripping it in his own powerful fingers.

Slocum didn't have to think about it. He'd done all his thinking ahead of time, while he waited, and now it was just fast, sure action. He grabbed the hand and yanked on it, pulling the door open and stepping around with his Colt in his left fist. He heard a startled "Hey!" and then came face to face with a young deputy clawing for his gun. The boy was no more than nineteen and scared out of his wits. Slocum hit him on the neck with the butt of the Colt, stunning him. He planted his other fist neatly on the man's chin, sending him reeling back into the barn. Slocum stepped in after him and shut the door.

He heard the sound of three shots booming outside, somewhere behind the barn and maybe up on the hill. Someone had been watching everything, he thought. He scowled in the dark, knowing his one consolation was that he hadn't made a target of himself coming into the stable. And at least he didn't have to kill the boy who was now struggling to get up off the ground.

There was no light in the barn. He only heard a rustling in the hay and gravel. He shifted his Colt into his right hand and quickly reached down with his left, feeling along the boy's body for his head. When he found it he held his fingers there, held the boy's skull in place, and tapped it gently again with the Colt. The boy lay still.

Slocum knew his horses were somewhere just to his left, and he almost felt rather than saw the opening of the stall. Only one animal was saddled—he couldn't explain the other one where he was going—and now he felt underneath the pony's belly to check the rigging. He felt the ropes and cinches hastily, and as far as he could tell no one had tampered with his horse. His warbag was still on the saddle, and so was the Henry rifle.

He didn't have time for more checking. He heard running feet along the far wall of the barn. It sounded like only one man, so far, heading for the back. Slocum mounted and rode toward the front, counting on his little horse to shy away from any barriers. He knew the liveryman was somewhere inside, but he didn't expect any more trouble from that one. He probably figured he'd done enough interfering for one night.

Slocum saw lines of gray, cracks between the big swinging doors at the front. He leaned down from the saddle, feeling for the latch and softly sliding it back. He took one deep breath, making a noise when he blew it out. Then he pushed the door wide and kicked his horse into a run.

Slocum saw two men racing toward him along the street. He hunkered low in the saddle and turned off into an alley just as the men opened fire. Another man appeared ahead of him, at the other end of the alley, blazing away with a rifle. Slocum felt the slugs singing by, too close for comfort. He worried for the horse, offering such a broad target, and he snapped off two quick shots on the run. The man with the rifle spun away without a sound and disappeared. Slocum ran the horse on into the street with his Colt still up, but he saw the gunman sprawled on the boardwalk, moaning and gripping his leg.

This street was clear, but he was back in the middle of the gulch with too many hiding places and too much distance between himself and the safety of the woods. He also knew the others would be mounted in a few more minutes.

Slocum kept his pony running and chose another alley at random, taking the turns at full speed and coming out into another street nearer the creek. He saw muzzle flashes off to the right and a moment later heard the booming of a rifle and a shotgun. As the sound rolled away there came the sound of slugs thunking into logs. Slocum had already wheeled into another alley, running his hand along the horse's flanks. It came away smeared with blood. He patted the horse on the neck. "Almost out," he whispered.

He was just coming out of the alley when he caught a flicker of movement to his right. He fired from his hip and the man screamed, grabbing his midsection and letting a heavy gun of some kind clatter to the boardwalk.

Slocum ground his teeth together, grimly furious. Most of the men who worked for Swearingen, and maybe even the marshal, would deserve what they got. But some of them might not have known any better.

Slocum hoped he hadn't killed one of them—or wouldn't have to.

All the time he'd been loose Slocum had been angling back toward Whitewood Creek and the road up Strawberry Hill. Now he made a flat-out run down into the creek bed and headed south, turning his horse toward the most level ground he could find. The pony's hooves slipped in the loose gravel just as Slocum's feet had done, but they kept moving. After a few hundred yards Slocum urged the horse back up the bank onto the stage road, just where it left town. He saw the muzzle flames of another rifleman up on the hillside, maybe the same one that had given the alarm, but the range was too great for Slocum to worry about. He kept himself folded low over the neck of his horse, knowing that he would present only a shadowy form to the distant shooter.

Slocum glanced back down the road the way he had come. There was still no sign of pursuit, though he knew they would come. The ones who'd survived the night would find their animals and saddle them and get organized. They probably weren't more than five minutes behind, Slocum figured, but the little spotted pony between his legs was hardly lathered yet. He felt the flanks again and found only a few scratches, the blood already starting to dry.

The little pony pounded on, out of sight of the rifleman on the hillside, and Slocum nodded with satisfaction. He'd outrun

the bastards for sure. He was hardly thinking of them anymore,
except to regret that Butcher wasn't among the men that he'd
shot on the way out. Slocum shrugged.

There would be a time...

18

By mid-afternoon of the next day Slocum had found his way to a granite ledge two hundred feet above the Deep Springs stage station. He crawled carefully to the rim and lay there, enjoying the mild late-May sun that gently warmed his back. He felt a bit like a rattlesnake sunning himself on the rocks— and he felt just as deadly when he started to think about Merry Atwood in the hands of Bill Chambers.

If she was.

Slocum had managed to stay away from Swearingen's men with a couple of midnight side trips into heavy timber, skirting one meadow and crossing a high boulder field. He had started out on the well-traveled freight road that drops straight south from Deadwood, then struck due east. But after obscuring his trail he followed a stream that recrossed the road, heading west toward the stage highway that looped around toward Wyoming Territory. He stayed with the stream a ways, following it up into a narrow canyon, and there he drank thirstily—just upstream from his pony. Then he had gone off from the noisy stream and staked his horse in a small patch of grass close by, bedding down against a rock overhang for a chilly and restless four hours of sleep.

By day Slocum had kept to the woods, bypassing the occasional ranch or miner's camp. From an aspen grove on a hillside he caught a glimpse of Butcher about mid-morning, trotting his fagged horse back along the freight road to Deadwood. Butcher looked not only tired but angry. Slocum saw it as a warning. He had taken a heavy toll on Swearingen's forces, and it wasn't likely that the Gem crowd would be giving up anytime soon.

Not long afterward Slocum had come across another of the many canyons in this broken country, but he also saw the well-worn game trails that suggested this canyon wouldn't be a dead end. Instead the floor lifted gradually for about five miles, the granite walls slowly closing in, until he came to a place where his little spotted pony could scramble up through a narrow cut to a grass plateau. The grass was rich and green and tall, stretching away on gentle slopes beneath scattered pines and a few burr oak. The breeze on top whispered in the pines, and Slocum once again was aware of the smell that was like perfume. For much of the afternoon he had continued angling cross-country. When he finally came onto the stage road he stopped to examine the surroundings before he could decide, based on his ride down with Horatio Brown, that he was still a mile or two above Deep Springs. He had turned south, again keeping to the trees and rocks beside the road.

Now a full half hour of observation from the ledge had shown no sign of activity at the station below. Slocum counted eight horses in the corral, the big powerful grays that the stage line liked to use. He also saw a couple head of oxen, which puzzled him. Perhaps they were left behind by a freighter, or one of the pilgrims using the road. No horses were tied up out front of the little cabin, and Rousseau never showed his face. Everything looked quiet, which was just the way Slocum liked it. He backed away from the edge of the rock and was about to swing into his saddle when he thought to wonder what day it was. When he'd finished counting back he took his foot from the stirrup and resettled himself on the ground, leaning against a pine tree that seemed to grow out of solid granite.

It was Saturday. The Cheyenne stage would be along in an hour or two.

Slocum was there on the outcrop to see it come jangling in, raising a trail of dust that he could see for twenty minutes before it arrived—a smoky trail of billowing clouds that glowed orange in the last rays of the sun, floating above deep-green pines. He watched the passengers climb down—three men and two women, this time—and walk the stiffness out of their joints. He watched them eat big plates of hot food while he made do with a tough piece of jerky. He watched Rousseau, or Chambers, unhitch a tired pair of horses from the coach and take them off for their rest after the fifteen-mile run from the last station up the line. And he watched two fresh grays led into their place. Rousseau buckled the rigging around their great muscular necks and bellies. The horses seemed to dance in excitement.

Slocum didn't see the stage leave. He was already in the saddle, picking his way off the ledge in dusky twilight. He circled the station from the south and tied his horse to a tree in a sheltered hollow of rock, where the scent wouldn't reach the stage animals in the corral. Slocum became a silent shadow in the pines, which took him within forty feet of the log cabin. He smelled wood smoke and saw the wisps of it above the mud-and-stone chimney. From the edge of the forest he watched the cabin. There was one window in its side, and the light of an oil lamp flickered there. No one came or went. The horses behind the cabin were settled.

Slocum slipped his Navy from its holster and spun the cylinder in the last cold light from a gray sky. All caps in place. All balls secure. He padded across the last few feet of grass, circling away from the window to come up along the front wall. He crept along the wall to the sagging plank door and cocked his ear, listening. He thought he heard the clunk of a dish set on a table. Slocum raised his boot in front of him and kicked the door. It slapped inward on its hinges and Slocum's momentum brought him in right behind.

Rousseau was spooning some stew into a bowl on the rough boards of a makeshift table. His head came up and he glanced at Slocum, at the gun in Slocum's hand, and then at the door. He shook his head and filled the rest of the bowl.

"It was open," he complained. "Now yuh gone an' busted my goddamn latch."

Slocum looked at the door, caught by surprise.

"If yuh think I'm gonna give you any of this stew," said Rousseau, "you can just go fuck yourself." He carried the black iron kettle back toward the fireplace and set it down in front of the flames. He licked his lips, then his mouth almost disappeared again in his black curly beard. He scratched himself and looked plaintively at Slocum. "Don't see why you had to bust my latch."

Slocum almost laughed. He felt a little foolish standing there with his Colt, because Rousseau was not impressed. Other men were supposed to be scared of you if you were waving a gun in their face. Slocum almost laughed, and then it made him nervous that the stationmaster seemed so confident. Slocum shut the door behind him and jammed a chair against it. He scanned the small room carefully but found no hiding places. He stayed to one side, out of sight of the single window.

"If I want some of your stew I'll take it," Slocum said roughly. "When I get through you'll wish that's all I wanted."

Rousseau was sitting at the table now. "So you're the one what's been up on the ridge," he whined. "Christ, yuh could make a man jumpy that way."

Slocum frowned, keeping his eyes on the stationmaster.

"Oh hell," said the man, lifting his bearded chin toward the pot. "If it'll make you feel better get yourself some stew."

"Get away from the table," Slocum said.

"Now wait a minute!"

"Stop whining and get away from the goddamn table."

The stationmaster's eyes turned hard, and for a moment he didn't move. He stared at Slocum's Colt. Slowly he stood, hands slightly away from his side, and stepped back from his table.

"Middle of the room," said Slocum.

The man moved back, reluctantly, as Slocum came on. Slocum studied the tabletop. He lifted a cup that had been turned over. He patted the cloth covering. Finally he reached beneath the table and felt with his hand. It stopped suddenly when he found the butt of a revolver. He slipped the gun out and put it on the table so he could feel the piece of leather that had held it there. The improvised holster had been nailed to the bottom of the table. Slocum pocketed the hideout gun, an ugly short-barreled revolver with the sight and the hammer filed off.

"Now you can eat," said Slocum, stepping back.

Rousseau's small black eyes glared at him as he sat down, but in a moment they lost their sharpness and took on their original puppy-dog look. "Man's got to have protection," he said. "Can't hardly blame me for that, can yuh, mister?"

"'Course not."

Rousseau glanced at him again. "What d'yuh want, anyway? I ain't told the comp'ny your real name, if that's it."

Slocum felt a quick chill before he understood. "So you do remember?" he said.

"El Paso? Shit yes. It ain't every day I get locked up with a horse thief and a killer." The black eyes suddenly dropped to Slocum's gun. The man tried a sickly smile. "Naturally I'm jess' talkin' about what they claimed yuh done."

"Naturally."

Rousseau licked his lips again.

"Unfortunately for you," Slocum said easily, "they weren't so far from wrong."

The stationmaster couldn't help himself. His glance jerked toward the back of the cabin, where the corrals lay. He pushed his chair back. "Not the grays," he whined.

"Yup."

"Now look, mister, you can't do that."

"Why the hell not?" Slocum yelled, apparently in a sudden rage. "This stage company is guilty of false arrest, isn't it? They threatened me with hanging, didn't they? And when I try to get away they try to fill my hide with buckshot!" Slocum's voice was almost out of control. "Damn it, I got it comin' to me."

Rousseau stood up, his hands pleadingly in front of him. "None of that was my fault, was it? Yuh can't blame me."

"You work for 'em."

"That's just it, Lacey."

So that was the name I used in El Paso, Slocum thought. Now if only I could remember the rest of it.

"It's just a job for me," Rousseau was saying. "But think how it will look if I let you take the horses."

That's exactly what Slocum had been thinking of. He had decided to pressure the stationmaster by threatening to stir things up for him and the gang he supposedly fronted for. He might think that a theft at his own station would point suspicion in his direction. It was ass-backwards thinking, of course, but then the average badman was no great thinker.

"My reputation," whined the bearded man. "It'll make me look bad." He was slowly working his way toward Slocum as he pleaded with him.

"Don't worry about your reputation," Slocum said shortly. "You'll be dead."

"Dead!" He took a step closer. "Why, mister? What have yuh got against me?"

"You've seen too much. You know who I am."

"You think I'd tell?"

Slocum nodded, and almost smiled bitterly when he put himself in the stationmaster's shoes. It would seem a strange twist of fate for an outlaw to die at the hands of another outlaw who was afraid of being informed on.

"You're makin' a bad mistake," said Rousseau. "Believe me, you'll be sorry." He took another step closer. "Everyone knows them horses. Yuh can't hide the brands. You'll never be able to sell 'em." Another step. "An' I'll be kilt, all for nothing."

"Sorry," Slocum said with a shrug. "Get down on the floor and I'll make it easy on you."

The stationmaster looked desperate, and Slocum knew some of what was in his mind. The Colt Navy was a single-action, uncocked in Slocum's hand. It might take a precious moment to thumb the hammer back, and a man can do a lot in a moment like that. Especially when he has no other choice or hope. Slocum knew, and yet, even knowing, he had been lulled by the man's complaints and his whining.

The bearded man started to turn away, which was when Slocum expected something, but he never expected Rousseau to move so quickly. The man spun on his heel and grabbed Slocum's Colt with his right hand almost at the same time that he threw a credible punch with his left. Slocum ducked at the last instant and winced when he caught the solid blow on his neck. Rousseau yanked on the Colt, but Slocum held his grip. Now he felt the barrel of the gun being bent toward his belly. When he resisted he found that the stationmaster's tattered woolen shirt hid hard muscle. Slocum balled his hand and hit Rousseau in the eye. The man's head snapped back, but he kept the pressure on. There was no sound in the little cabin except the faint sputtering of the oil lamp and the strained breathing of two powerful men. The Colt was suspended between them, unmoving.

Suddenly Rousseau tried to bring his knee up between Slocum's legs. Slocum turned slightly and deflected it with his thigh. At that instant Rousseau turned in the same direction Slocum had been going and arched his arms up over their heads, trying to twist the gun from Slocum's hands. This time the momentum carried them around so that they were back to back. Rousseau was struggling fiercely—struggling for his life— and it suddenly came to Slocum that he had better get serious. The man would think nothing of killing Slocum if he could.

Slocum turned his body again, and the two men completed their pirouette, but as soon as they were face to face Slocum lowered his eyes and butted Rousseau's forehead. Their skulls knocked loudly, and Rousseau groaned. Slocum followed through by lifting his boot and stomping the top of Rousseau's foot. There was a sharp intake of breath through gritting teeth, but the grip on Slocum's gun was still there.

"Damn it all," said Slocum. "What does it take?"

Rousseau's face had lost its color, but now he was like a mad cat, clawing and gouging and landing blows wherever he could with his left hand. Slocum stayed busy fending him off. Then in the confusion he felt a grab for his coat pocket, and before Slocum could react Rousseau had slipped out the little gun that had been underneath the table.

It came out nice and easy with such a short barrel and no sights or hammer to catch on. Rousseau shoved. The two men broke apart, Slocum already thumbing back the hammer on his Navy. Rousseau didn't have to cock the double-action revolver. He aimed the gun, and, in a roar that filled the cabin he said, "Now *hold* it!"

Slocum was staring into the short little barrel and Rousseau was staring into the bigger barrel of the Colt. Slocum was silently thankful that the two of them were experienced men of the frontier. They could recognize a standoff. They knew they would both die, no matter who shot first. The two men stood four feet apart, tired muscles trembling slightly, their chests rising and falling in the dim light from the oil lamp. Their faces ran with sweat, and Slocum could smell that Rousseau hadn't bathed recently. The stationmaster licked his lips and repeated himself.

"Now hold on one damn minute here."

He was still catching his breath.

"We gonna stand like this forever?" Slocum said. "I feel like maybe we oughta get married. You think this is what it's like?"

Rousseau didn't smile. Slocum didn't think he'd ever seen him smile, for that matter. "Now hear me out," the station-master said. He took a couple more deep breaths, and a little of the whining tone came back into his voice. "Yuh don't want to kill me, mister. That'd be stupid. We're more or less on the same side, you' n' me."

"What?"

"That ain't bullshit, neither. I know a little something about a gang that operates round here, see? And they sometimes can use a man what knows how to handle himself."

"I work alone."

Rousseau made a tiny motion with the little gun. "Yuh ain't never gonna work again, maybe."

"Since you put it that way—"

"It's stupid, is what it is. Penny ante bullshit."

"This bunch knows what it's doing, huh?"

"From what I seen, yeah. But talk to the boss."

"Who's that?"

"He'll be along." Rousseau's black eyes glittered. "He'll be along pretty quick, I expect."

Which explained a little of the man's first lack of worry, thought Slocum. "You mean tonight?" he said aloud.

Rousseau nodded. "He'll tell yuh his name if he wants yuh to know it. I ain't promisin' nothing, understand. Just to introduce yuh."

Slocum narrowed his eyes. "You think I'm a fool?" he said. "You think I'll believe this story and drop my gun, just so you can shoot me?"

"I'm tellin' yuh it's true. But what about me, mister? I take your word that you'll think on it, and then you shoot *me*."

"How about we lower these things together," said Slocum, "nice an' easy, and put them away."

Rousseau nodded and then he said, "Ready?"

"Yeah."

The two men started lowering their guns inch by slow inch,

unblinking eyes locked together. With guns at their sides Slocum and Rousseau eased them simultaneously into holster and
behind waistband. Their hands stayed on the grips an instant,
then floated slowly away at the stationmaster's nod.

"I guess now we wait," said Slocum. "Can you eat left-
handed?"

The stationmaster nodded again and they shuffled sideways
toward the table, arms hanging strangely away from their sides.
They sat down slowly, and Slocum put both forarms on the
table. Rousseau laid his right arm on the table and gripped the
spoon with his left hand, awkwardly bringing the food to his
lips while he kept his eyes more or less on Slocum's body,
alert for sudden movement.

Slocum felt it coming, and he said, "Don't get scared but
I got to laugh now." He laughed out loud and a tear formed
in his eye and he shook his head. "Yeah," he said, "this is
getting more like marriage every minute."

"I wouldn't know," Rousseau said in a sour tone.

Slocum's humor died after a moment. "Yeah," he said.
"Well, now we wait."

19

"Been a while since El Paso," said the stationmaster.

"Yeah," said Slocum. "Long time."

It was their first conversation since the fight. They were still sitting at the rough wooden table, the oil lamp between them but just off to one side. Each man still had his arms out in front of him. The tin bowl in front of Rousseau had been empty for half an hour. A couple of early flies buzzed around it and settled on the rim. Rousseau blew them away, the hairs of his beard fluttering around his mouth.

"D'yuh go to trial, Lacey?"

"They started one," said Slocum. "When I saw how it was going I decided to broaden my horizons with travel."

The stationmaster nodded vaguely, staring off to one side. "Covered a lot of ground since then, I bet."

"Yeah."

Slocum frowned at Rousseau, trying to understand the questions. It could be a simple hunger to talk, but it could also be that the man was trying to find out more about his past. That would be a reasonable thing if the man were going to be recommending him to an outlaw leader. Slocum figured he'd play along—knowing he had a lot of experiences to talk about that would fit the role he was playing.

Rousseau blew the flies away from his bowl again, and fiddled with the spoon. "That Navy's a fine-lookin' piece," he said casually. "An' been around, too. You pick that up in the War Between the States?"

Slocum nodded. "Never could bring myself to part with it," he said, and smiled an evil smile. "Especially not after I used it to kill a judge that thought he could steal my land."

"Fucking judges," said Rousseau. "Southerner, then?"

"Yup. Calhoun County, Georgia."

"I'm out of Arkansas, myself, but I left before the war. Yuh ever try to live by the book?"

"When it seemed like a good idea," Slocum said carefully, and more or less truthfully. "But usually it doesn't work out that way for me."

Rousseau nodded thoughtfully. "Worked a runnin' iron, I suppose?"

"Yeah. Trailed my share of cows over the border. Tried a bank here and there."

Rousseau's head jerked up. "Banks!"

"When I was desperate, friend. And you have to be pretty hard up to tackle a bank. I generally stick to places where I don't plan to hang around after the wanted posters come out. I don't have anything to worry about in Dakota."

The stationmaster took a breath as if to say something else, but the sound of hooves came up the road.

Slocum's right hand slipped off the table and reappeared instantly with the Colt, the hammer eared back. Rousseau's hand was only halfway down to his own gun when he froze, frowning at Slocum's revolver as if he were trying to understand by what magic it came to be there.

"Now I know you claim this is gonna be that outlaw friend of yours," Slocum said. "But I'm alive right now because I don't take chances. And if I were you, friend, I wouldn't take any chances on trying to warn anyone."

The horse was close, and there was only one. Rousseau looked at Slocum's face and for the first time he smiled. Sort of. "Christ that was slick," he said. "I don't know if I've ever seen faster."

"Just let your hands rest easy, then. Keep them on the table and there won't be any problem."

Slocum stood up and backed toward the door, where he pulled away the chair he'd used to jam it shut. He carried the chair to the far corner of the little cabin, against the wall with the window, so that he couldn't be seen from the outside but could still command the dinner table and the door. The horse trotted to the front of the cabin. It sounded like a big man that jumped down and landed in the dirt. Rousseau looked at Slocum a moment and then both men had their eyes fixed on the entrance. They heard the sound of a wolf howl just outside as the door was swung open, and the man coming in said, "Gerry, that little blonde was the best thing you ever done for—"

The man stopped and stared. "What the fuck?" he said.

"Come on in and close the door," Slocum said evenly. "Join the party."

The new arrival was big all right. A couple of inches taller than Slocum and a good fifty pounds heavier, the kind of solid weight that's distributed evenly over heavy bones. Slocum tensed a little, recognizing that this was someone he wouldn't want to tangle with at all. He had black hair like his brother, without the beard, and the same small black eyes. When he first came in the eyes had held a humorous twinkle, and Slocum could understand the man's reputation for charm. But now the eyes were simply cold and mean.

"What's going on?" he said.

Rousseau smiled. "Come on in, Bill. Do as the man says. I think he might be useful."

Slocum looked at the stationmaster, acting surprised. "You saying this is Bill Chambers? The one they call Persimmon Bill?"

Rousseau was still smiling. "One an' the same," he said. "You heard of him?"

"Of course! It's a name to be reckoned with, in the circles I travel in."

"You still game, then?"

"More than ever," said Slocum, but he was still keeping the Colt in front of him.

The stationmaster turned to Bill Chambers, who had closed the door as best he could with the broken latch and was sidling his way into the room. "This fella," said Rousseau, "tells me he's interested in joining the gang. What do you think, Bill?"

The man rolled his big shoulders in a massive shrug. "How the fuck should I know? You're running things."

The stationmaster looked at Slocum again. "Yeah, I guess I am," he said. The whining tone had disappeared from his voice. "I guess I am at that."

Slocum's mind felt sluggish. "You mean *you're* the boss?"

"Yuh got it right, Lacey." The stationmaster was grinning. "The name's Gerry Chambers, by rights. And there ain't no way in hell I'd trust things to this crazy brother of mine."

20

Slocum set out late the next morning in the company of Bill Chambers, after a long night of drinking with his new partners in the little cabin by the stage road. The night had gotten louder as it got later, with bragging and tall tales, but Slocum sensed that he was still being watched and occasionally tested. He expected it and understood. The Chambers brothers could hardly ask for references. Instead they would rely as always on a keen animal instinct that told them whether this man Lacey, as they knew him, was one of *them*. There is often a feeling you get when you've come among those of your own kind, Slocum reflected, just as he himself felt at home in the badlands of Deadwood. Turning it over in his mind as he ambled north on the stage road, Slocum had the feeling that the Chambers brothers' instincts didn't often lead them astray. So if they accepted him into the gang . . . Slocum followed the line of thought for a minute or so, frowning, then shrugged and gave it up. He saw himself as a Georgia farm boy who had once wanted only to work the family place but got sidetracked. Somehow he had turned into the man who could drink easily with the likes of Bill and Gerry Chambers.

Slocum glanced at the hulking form of Chambers beside him and saw that the man's face was touched with the hint of a smile as he rode, for no apparent reason. And it was a happy smile. That was the difference between the two brothers, Slocum thought. The stationmaster had a gloomy nature that saw little humor, and even his rare smiles were mean and somehow cruel. He was driven by some dark force that his brother didn't have. That force had, of course, led him to success in his chosen field—only temporary, if Slocum had his way—while

113

his brother was content to trail along. But his brother at least had a good time doing it.

Chambers seemed to feel Slocum's gaze and turned to say, "Nice day, ain't it?"

"That sun sure feels good."

"Don't it? I was commencin' to think winter'd never end."

"You were up here the whole time?"

"Since December," Chambers said. "Almost as soon as the stage went through to Deadwood. Gerry, he was studyin' on it, an' he saw that the Injuns was on the run after they killed Custer. Sitting Bull's in Canada, they say, and the Army's about run down Crazy Horse. So Gerry, he says this is the prime time for our line o' work. 'Cause soon these hills'll be run over with people in every little meadow. He's prob'ly right, but right now we got a little roost all to ourselves."

"Your brother's a thinking man, I see."

"That's Gerry, all right."

"So what's our line of work?"

Bill Chambers frowned. "I guess you'll know when you need to know, Lacey. I ain't so sure I should talk."

"Whatever's right," said Slocum. "I just wondered what I was getting myself into."

For a minute or two there was only the sound of creaking saddle leather and the horses' hooves on the hard dirt road. Slocum had learned the night before not to press too hard, when the two brothers had pulled off to one side and started talking in low tones. Slocum had said he thought he was part of their crowd now, and Gerry Chambers had given him a sullen stare. "You'll know what you need to know," he'd said, "when you need to know it. Just like everyone else." Slocum had had the feeling that Bill Chambers was getting directions from his brother, and he wondered if it was not just coincidence that the meeting came on the night that the stage passed by. Slocum had started wondering how Gerry Chambers got his information, living in his isolation in the middle of the Black Hills. The more he thought about it, the more it seemed that a regular passenger or even a friendly driver or shotgun guard could be feeding him what he needed to know. It was something to look into later.

The two men had been on the road less than half an hour when Chambers suddenly slowed his horse and grinned at Slocum.

"Here't'is," he said cheerfully. "Here's where we head on into the robbers' roost."

Slocum knew that he was supposed to be surprised and puzzled. "I don't see any trail," he said.

Chambers' grin got bigger. "Who'd want ta leave a trail?" he said. "We got a highway, maybe, but no trail."

Slocum was thankful for the big man's playfulness. It gave him a chance to study the country and fix this place in his memory. From where he sat his horse, the graded road fell away into a grassy meadow thick with wildflowers that showed no sign of trampling. He eliminated the meadow. Directly to his right lay the forest, cool and shaded, but he also could see no sign of disturbance among the pine needles that carpeted the earth there. On his left the road had been skirting huge boulders of granite, thirty and forty feet high, but here the granite had dipped into a kind of saddle before flowing into a ridge that rimmed the grassy meadow to the west.

Slocum looked back at Chambers, who was still grinning as if he expected Slocum to give up any minute and admit he was stumped. Instead Slocum turned toward the low spot in the granite and kicked his horse up into the little notch.

"Hey!"

Slocum stopped his horse and turned.

"How'd you know?" said Chambers.

Slocum slowly looked down at the crusty mottled rock beneath his horse, then slowly back at Chambers, with a smile. "I ain't leavin' no trail, am I?"

Chambers shook his head. "Guess you're too smart for this ol' boy," he said good-naturedly, and followed Slocum into the notch.

"You could take a good-size herd through here," Slocum said.

"Herd of what?"

"You tell me."

Chambers frowned again. "I guess it wouldn't hurt. Hell, you probably figured most of it out already."

"Is the stage company losing a lot of horses?"

Chambers shook his head again. "Bingo," he said. "But that ain't all."

"No?" Slocum thought he could make a few more good guesses, but he decided to let Bill Chambers have some fun of his own. He could see that as the man's respect for him grew, the more Chambers wanted to impress him. He hadn't planned it, but he knew instinctively that it would be useful.

"Not by a long shot," said Chambers. "We're in the cattle business, too."

Now it was Slocum's turn to frown. "How's that?" he said. "There aren't but one or two little ranches within a hundred miles."

"Who said anything about ranches?"

Slocum touched his heels to his horse as the notch turned slightly and began climbing. He could see a covering of trees ahead.

"Of course!" Slocum said suddenly. "The reservations."

"Yup," said Chambers. "We're makin' sure the Red bastards don't get fat and sassy."

"You and the agent."

Chambers didn't say anything.

"So the U. S. of A. is supplying you with government-issue beef," said Slocum, as though he were marveling. "And thanks to you and the U.S. of A. the miners are getting fat and sassy instead of the Indians."

"Serves the bastards right."

"Yeah," said Slocum. "First we steal their land. Then we steal their food."

"Right!" said Chambers, and Slocum rolled his eyes. There wasn't much point in using sarcasm with Bill Chambers.

"Well it looks like I cut myself a rich piece of pie," Slocum said. "Here's 'how' to everything on four legs."

"But that *still* ain't all," Chambers said.

Slocum faced his partner and saw that he was struggling with himself. Slocum didn't push it, only cocking one eyebrow and letting the silence stretch on.

"Oh lordy," said Chambers, and he was almost shaking with some kind of excitement. "Don't say I told you, okay? Don't say nothing to nobody."

"Sure."

"We just heard, just now. The line's gonna start runnin' some kind of treasure coach!"

"Treasure coach?"

Chambers bobbed his head up and down. "There'll be people on it too, if they want. But it'll be carrying gold dust out of the hills. Think of it, Lacy! A whole goddamn safeful of gold ripe for the pickin'. And us here to pick it."

Slocum shook his head. "I'm thinking, Bill, and I'm thinking the damn thing will be pretty well guarded."

"Well of course! Why do you think my brother wants you in the gang? We need as many hardcases as we can get our hands on, men who can take care o' themselves in a tough situation."

Gerry Chambers had told his brother the night before of their struggle for Slocum's gun, and the speed of Slocum's draw when they'd heard his approaching horse.

"Look at las' night," Bill Chambers said now. "Not one man in a hundred would've thought to look 'neath the table. An' Gerry already told me about the day you escaped from ol' man Brown." Chambers laughed. "I'd love to of seen that one. Yeah, Lacey, you're the one for us."

"Well, thanks," said Slocum. "It still ain't gonna be easy. I just hope we don't have to split the take too many ways."

Chambers grinned. "Naw. Mebbe eight 'r nine. Depending on if everyone survives."

Slocum thought about the gang of outlaws he was about to meet, apparently five or six other men besides the Chambers brothers and whoever they were paying off in town to pass them information. He tried to imagine the hideout toward which he was riding—an isolated place where he'd be alone. Probably five other men like himself. And that's what made him nervous. The settlers and explorers came and went, he thought, but the ones who rode both sides of the law—the hardcases, as Chambers had called them—they were a smaller crowd. He wondered who might be there and whether one of them would recognize him as John Slocum. He knew he would have to be looking for an escape route even as they rode down into the robbers' roost.

He also had to remember there wouldn't be the time to do

this job the way he was supposed to. Horatio Brown wanted him to witness all the illegal activity, to see the thefts and payoffs, to discover their routes and their ultimate customers. But if the gang's Deadwood informant really was Al Swearingen, then Slocum knew that every hour he spent in the roost would be dangerous. One of the gang was sure to hear of the black-haired, green-eyed stranger who had caused so much trouble in town and start to put things together. Even worse would be a visit to the roost by one of Swearingen's hired guns. Once he was recognized, Slocum would have to move fast— if he hoped to get out of the roost alive.

Slocum's thinking circled back to the problem of time, and he decided to take a risk. "About that treasure coach," he said. "Was that in the paper or something?"

"I wouldn't know, Lacey."

"Then you're getting information from the inside, somehow."

Chambers' eyes were glittering. "That ain't none o' your business."

"Goddamn it," Slocum yelled. "I'm getting sick of everyone telling me to mind my own business!"

"Now look—"

"*You* look. Suppose you're getting a tip-off on this treasure coach. Now suppose the guy tipping you off really works for the company."

"You're thinkin' it could be a trap?"

"It's possible. It can happen. And I don't want to walk into any traps on another man's say-so." Slocum was quieting down, but he was still speaking harshly. "That's why it's my business, Chambers. I gotta decide who I'm gonna trust."

Bill Chambers was looking either thoughtful or mean. Slocum couldn't tell which. "Well, you don't have to worry about that," he finally said. "My brother's the smart one."

"I hope so," said Slocum. "Just don't keep telling me to mind my own business."

Slocum and Chambers had come off the cap rock and ridden into the pines. Every once in a while he could see the meadow off to his right, and he had the feeling they were circling around behind it.

"I guess your brother'd have to be pretty tricky at that," said Slocum, "to manage getting himself hired by the company to begin with."

Chambers grinned. "That's just it, Lacey. That's the thing. If Gerry says somethin', you know it's so."

"How'd he get the name Rousseau?"

The outlaw's grin turned crafty. "You might say he picked it up along the way," said Chambers. "That ol' boy who use'ta own the name, he ain't around to protest anymore."

Slocum shuddered and fell into silence. After another hour they came into a small clearing and Slocum noticed that the sun was almost behind them now, meaning they had gradually turned north. After the clearing the land sloped gently downward, and in another mile they were angling along a grassy hillside.

Here he saw the trails of grass bent beneath the hooves of many animals and other riders. He had noticed a few marks in the pine needles, too, but there were many ways to come off the cap rock. Even if a posse had explored that far, it would be hard to find a trail leading in any definite direction. In the far distance Slocum could see the dry plains of Wyoming Territory. Directly ahead, however, were soft-shaped hills and grassy ravines with a couple dozen antelope raising their heads for a curious look before running off a few yards to graze and look some more. Up above, the slopes were rimmed by more forest. Chambers led the way into one of the ravines, and Slocum tried to mark it from the others—tried to imagine where he was in relation to the stage road and Deadwood. He wasn't sure anymore.

When they were back in the trees, climbing again, Chambers looked at Slocum and licked his lips, the way his brother had.

"I can't hardly wait to get back," he said. "Never thought I'd say so about that godforsaken hole, but here I am sayin' it."

"I can guess why," Slocum said, forcing a grin.

"I bet you can, Lacey. But you won't know the half of it till you seen her!"

The brothers had talked loud and long the night before about their new blonde. They had called her Merry Merry, and Bill

Chambers had described some of the things she was forced to do. Slocum's jaws still ached a bit from the way his teeth were grinding.

"Will I get that chance?" said Slocum.

"To see her? Sure." Chambers leered at him. "As for anything besides lookin' . . . I guess you'll have ta wait till I'm done. I'll get her good an' broken in for you."

It was a moment before Slocum could trust himself to speak, and then he wasn't sure whether he was goading Chambers or putting salt on an open cut. "Figure everyone else will be done with her by the time we get back?"

Chambers laughed. "Sure!" he said. "Two or three times around. Won't be no fights out there for a while, that much I can tell you. Those boys'll be too busy fuckin' to get on each other's nerves."

"Unless one of them takes a particular shine to her."

"Ain't much chance of that, Lacey."

"You just got done telling me what a looker she was."

"A looker, yeah, but mean as a rattlesake. Brother! You gotta knock the little bitch around jus' to get it in 'er."

"Not the willing type, huh?"

"That's the way she plays it," Chambers said with a shrug. "But of course she ain't gettin' paid. That's all."

"Then how'd she get to be there?" said Slocum. He was playing dumb because the Chambers brothers had never been specific about how the blonde came to be in the robbers' roost.

Chambers shrugged. "She made someone mad."

"I'm not sure I like that, Bill. What if someone's looking for her?"

"Don't worry, friend. She was just a whore in Deadwood that made somebody mad, and that's all there is to it. No one's lookin' for her."

"Except me," said Slocum, adding a knowing grin after a moment. "It's been too long since I had any."

"You'll git all you want, Lacey. Jus' as soon as I gentle 'er down for you."

Slocum didn't answer that one, and in a few minutes he thought he saw a break in the trees ahead. Suddenly they were on the edge of a large bowl formed by a limestone ledge on the far side and steep grassy hills the rest of the way around. Slocum assumed they had passed some sort of lookout on the way in, but the man had not made himself known. It was even possible the gang didn't feel the need for one, as isolated and free from pursuit as they seemed to be.

"There's your new home," Chambers said.

They pulled up at the top of a well-worn trail that cut across the hillside, looking down at a pair of poorly built cabins beside a small stream that ran through the bottom of the bowl. Slocum could see that someone had thrown up a little dam of rocks and sticks in the stream to form a small pond. Maybe a dozen horses were clustered there, drinking the water. Five of them were big grays, like the ones used by the stage line. There were a couple of grullas, one Morgan, and even a spotted pony like Slocum's.

In the far corner of the bowl, under a cloud of dust and smoke, wranglers were sorting out and branding a small herd of cattle. It looked like a regular ranch roundup to Slocum, except that even from the ridge he could see how long it took to use the branding iron, and the fact that it wasn't a simple matter of applied pressure. He could see, in other words, that the wranglers were using a running iron. He decided to get a closer look at the operation and a few of the brands before they were changed. He started down, and Chambers followed.

"Looks like the boys are back," Chambers said.

"Meaning we got some miserable work cut out for us."

Chambers laughed. "Wait'll you taste the cookin', Lacey. You jus' might up an' resign before the day is out."

"You accept resignations?"

Chambers gave Slocum a level, suspicious look. "I wouldn' like it so much."

"Don't worry, Bill. I got a hankerin' for blondes and gold dust, so if you've got the one and you're promising the other, that's enough to make me stick for a while."

"That's the way to talk."

"I also want to find out why they call you Persimmon Bill."

Chambers shook his head, then he grinned. "I wouldn' hold my breath on that one, partner." He nudged his horse, and they started down the side. It was the only trail Slocum could see as he scanned the rim of the big bowl, but he figured his little mountain-bred horse could climb either of the other two slopes. The only problem was that he and Merry would be sitting targets all the way up. It was wide-open country, and the climb toward the cover of the trees would be a long and hard one. They'd have to have a decent head start, and that was assuming there were no lookouts on the rim itself. *Damn it,* Slocum thought, *why can't things ever be simple?*

As the trail took them deeper and deeper into the bowl, Slocum had an image in his mind of the jaws of a big bear trap. They way he saw it, they were slowly closing above his head.

21

Slocum and Chambers splashed through the little creek, and the work around the branding fire came to a halt. Five men stood or sat their saddles in various poses—all hostile, Slocum thought—and watched the two of them ride up. Slocum made a quick study of their faces, but none were familiar. He breathed a little easier.

Chambers nodded his head. "Glad to see you back, Evans. Charley. Where's Parker?"

The outlaw standing by the fire with the branding iron in his hand took a step forward. "Went to town," he said. "Oughta be back tomorrow. With a little whiskey and some real food."

"Sound's good." Chambers glanced at the bellowing cattle. "How many'd we get?"

The man with the branding iron made a point of looking at Slocum, and Chambers said, "Oh. This here's Lacey. New man."

The man said, "Shit," and turned away.

"Relax, Quince. There'll be plenty to go around."

The one named Quince turned back and threw the running iron on the ground. "Right now all we got plenty of is work."

"Quince," said Chambers, in a warning tone.

Slocum climbed down from his horse and picked up the hot iron. "Let's get it over with," he said.

After a dinner of soured beef and tasteless beans Slocum sat on a log in front of the cabin door. He thought about the government brands he'd seen on the cattle that afternoon, and what he could testify to so far. He also thought about Parker, who was in Deadwood and due back the next day. While Slocum was thinking, Chambers pushed out the door and swaggered over toward the other cabin. Almost immediately Slocum heard the sound of a woman crying, and the sound of heavy blows. Slocum got up and stared tight-lipped in the direction of the sounds for a moment. Then he went back inside the main building.

The five outlaws were still seated around a table and a card game. No one looked up when he came in, but Slocum thought something had changed. They were quieter, as if he'd interrupted their talk. Or maybe they were waiting for something. Slocum figured he was in no hurry to see what it was, and in the meantime he'd pick out one of the bunks and stow his gear. The bunks were only a series of wooden platforms covered by some straw and a piece of cloth, surrounded by saddlebags and boots and other personal items that marked them as being used. But two of them looked empty, so Slocum picked up his warbag and bedroll from the corner near the front door and moved toward the bunk that looked the most comfortable.

"That's one's taken," said Quince.

Slocum hesitated, noticing the tense silence that had fallen over the table. "Excuse me," he said cheerfully. "I couldn't tell."

"That's your problem, Lacey, not mine."

"What about this one over here?"

"That's taken too." The one named Quince hadn't turned around. He was staring at the other outlaws from beneath the rim of his hat, and Slocum could imagine the satisfied smirk on his face. "They're all taken," he said.

A scream of pain, quickly stifled, came from the next cabin.

Slocum took a deep breath and said, "Do you have some ghosts in this gang? Maybe they're sleeping on these bunks right now and we're disturbing them."

"Yeah," said Quince. "Yeah, we got some gents we ain't never seen. Actually, we're all ghosts down here." There was some laughter around the table, and then Quince looked at Slocum. "Tell you what, Lacey, why don't you sit in for a few hands. Try your luck in a little five-card stud."

Slocum saw a couple of the other men glance up expectantly,

and he had an idea of what was coming. "Sure," he said lightly. "Deal me in." He saw a two-foot log section in a corner and turned it on its edge to roll it toward the table while the bandits finished the hand they were on. Once he was seated he put a hand in his coat pocket and slipped a few of the gold certificates from the dead pilgrim's wallet. Slocum didn't bother counting it, since he knew how much he'd started with. He had that figure commited to memory.

A couple of the men stared at the little stack of scrip with hungry eyes. They each had a poke of gold dust in front of them, and calling and raising bets was a matter of adding a pinch of the dust to a tin pie plate in the center of the table. That was the pot. The winner got to dump the contents of the pie plate back in his poke.

It was obvious from the beginning that Slocum wasn't meant to be one of the winners, and the men weren't too subtle about it. When their hands were poor and Slocum's had any chance of being good, they folded early. He had the second deal after he sat down, then it passed to a brown-haired youngster and then to a slightly older man with a scar beneath one eye before the deal got back to the one named Quince.

Quince grinned as he shuffled and said, "How 'bout we raise the ante a bit?"

Everyone looked at Slocum, who said, "How much?"

"A dollar to start?"

Slocum found a dollar and tossed it in. The other men measured out a slightly larger pinch. Quince was still shuffling the cards.

"Anytime," said Slocum.

The first round gave him an ace of clubs for his hole card, and the second round gave him an ace of diamonds showing.

"What does the ace bet?" Quince said.

"Another dollar, I suppose."

Slocum thought the dealer looked disappointed. Quince raised by two, with a four of hearts showing. He gave himself a four of spades on the next round and Slocum an eight of clubs. Two of the bandits dropped out, and the other two weren't showing anything of interest. Quince upped the bet by three dollars— just enough to keep Slocum in the game, hoping for another ace. On the fourth round he got it. Quince laid a king on top of his two fours.

Slocum made a show of checking his hole card and studying Quince's hand, as if he could read something there. Finally he grinned happily and said, "What the hell! We'll steal it all back this summer, right?" He found a ten-dollar bill and tossed it on the pie plate. Another bandit bowed out. Now it was obvious that the fourth one was working on a possible flush. All five outlaws were very still, their faces closing in, and the only sound was the slip of a card off the deck and the slap as it was laid down.

"Sorry, Joe," said the dealer. "There goes your flush."

The one called Joe looked disgusted, and without waiting for the bet he scooped up his cards and turned them over. It looked as though he'd really hoped to win—as if this weren't a setup.

"Uh oh," said Quince. "The new man pulls another eight."

Slocum had all he could do to keep a straight face. He had seen the dealer's moves, as skillful as they were, but he hadn't realized just how his own hand was shaping up until that moment.

"Well, what do you know," he said aloud. "This just might be the dead man's hand."

Quince was about to deal himself the last card. He froze. "What's that, Lacey?"

"Aces over eights," said Slocum.

The faces around him were blank. Their eyes were glittering, but the faces showed no other expression.

"You know," said Slocum. "The hand Hickock was holding last August when he was killed. 'Course, his was a full house. I ain't so sure what mine'll turn out to be."

"Ain't that a coincidence," said the dealer.

"Yeah," said Slocum, and his hand leaped across the table like a striking rattlesnake. He gripped the dealer's wrists in his hands. "Except you dealt it to the wrong man, Quince."

Slocum saw a movement out of the corner of his eye, one of the other men moving in. Slocum let go of one wrist, savagely backhanded the interfering bandit, and gripped the wrist again so fast that Quince didn't have time to react.

"I'll kill the next man that moves," said Slocum. "This is between me and him."

"You got no call—"

"Shut up, Quince. Let's make it double or nothing. I'll bet the whole pot that your hole card's a four."

Slocum's little finger arced out from the rest of the fingers around the dealer's wrist and flipped the card face up. It was a four of diamonds.

"So now the pot is mine, and—"

"Bullshit," said Quince. "You can't—"

Slocum squeezed harder, and the dealer's face contorted in pain.

"—and what I'll do," he continued coldly, "is bet the whole pot against whatever you got left in your poke that the next card off the bottom is a four of clubs."

"Off the bottom? You accusin' me of cheating?"

"You're catchin' on." Slocum twisted the dealer's left hand in a slow circle, turning the deck of cards upside down. Through Quince's clenched fingers he saw the four of clubs. Slocum gave a sound of disgust and let go, reaching for Quince's poke on the table in front of him.

But Quince was reaching for his holster, opening his mouth to yell something in his fury. Slocum had just gripped the butt of his own Colt when he heard a bellowing voice from the door: "Now *hold on!*"

All movement stopped. The other bandits had been getting on their feet to get out of the way. Slocum and Quince both had their guns out of their holsters. They all became statues, it seemed, Slocum and Quince glaring at each other, watching for the first twitch of a muscle that would keep things going.

Bill Chambers ambled through the door, still hitching up his pants. He wiped some sweat off his forehead.

"For chrissake, Quince, you oughta know better than ta brace a stranger. I jus' saved your damn life, boy!"

"I can take him."

"Not this one. Believe me. An' even if you did, he'd kill you as he fell. An' here we'd be two hands short. Now you keep the pot, Lacey—"

"Damn it, Bill."

"—an' Quince, you keep your poke. Now you boys put those guns away. If you still wanna fight in the mornin', you can use your fists."

"Be a pleasure."

"In the mornin', Quince."

"Anytime."

"Okay. Right now I got something I wanna show Lacey." Chambers beckoned with a tilt of his chin and Slocum followed him out of the cabin, cursing the luck that had kept him from cutting down the odds against him by one.

There was a chill in the air now that the sun was gone. Slocum caught up with Chambers and noticed in the murky twilight that the man looked a little worried.

"I don' know," said Chambers. "You're gonna have to learn how to make friends with that bunch."

"Maybe it'll be better when you tell them about the treasure coach. They'll stop worrying about losing a share."

"Mebbe. Anyway, you might as well stay out of their hair for a bit. An' I got jus' the right thing to keep you occupied."

They had been moving toward the other cabin. Now Chambers suddenly pushed open the door and pulled Slocum in by the arm. It was dark inside, but Slocum immediately recognized Merry Atwood. She was a broken-looking figure sprawled on a bunk, her eyes closed. She was naked, and she didn't care. When she heard the door she opened her eyes with a dull, resigned look, until she saw Slocum. He saw the recognition come slowly, but before she could open her mouth he was talking to Chambers.

"Well, I got to give you credit as a judge of feminine flesh," he said loudly. "No sir, Bill, I haven't seen such beauty in a long time. Maybe never." Slocum tried to give her a warning look, and either she understood or she was simply too dazed and confused to respond. She stared at him with a look of terror in her eyes.

"So get the hell out of here!" Slocum said to Chambers, in a friendly way. "Leave a man in peace."

Chambers grinned at Slocum, then at Merry. "You be a good girl, now. Understand?"

She cringed away from him, trying to make herself small,

and Slocum felt cold at the sight of Chambers' face when the grin went away.

"She understands," Chambers said harshly, but with a gleam of something like satisfaction in his eyes. "Oh yeah, she understands."

22

Slocum took two long steps toward the door just as it closed
and listened for the sound of Chambers going away. He thought
he heard the scuffling of boots in the grass, but he wasn't sure.
A moment later came the slap of the door on the other cabin.
Slocum chanced a small opening in his own door and then a
larger one. He didn't see anything outside.

With the other door closed again it was very dark in the
cabin. It had been built without windows, and the only light
came from a poor oil lamp sitting on a bench. Slocum saw two
candle stubs, but he figured they wouldn't last long. He shook
the lamp to see how much oil was left. Two or three hours,
anyway.

The girl was sitting up on the bunk. She had drawn her
knees up in front of her, and she was watching every move
Slocum made. When he glanced her way she gave him a pleading look. "Please don't hurt me," she begged. "I didn't know.
I'll do—"

Slocum put a finger to his lips. "Don't worry," he whispered. "You're safe now. No one will touch you again." There
was a rumpled blanket on the ground at the foot of the bunk.
Slocum picked it up and tossed it toward the girl. "Here," he
said. "Cover up."

Slocum picked the lamp off the bench and made a tour of
the four cabin walls, carefully inspecting the spaces between
the logs. Some of the mud chinking had fallen out, as he'd
expected, but only one of the holes would be large enough to
see through from the outside. He found a water pail that had
been left for the girl and tipped a handful of it into the dirt
floor, stirring it in to produce a paste. When it was thick enough

he slopped the mud paste into the hole. He poured a little more water onto his hands and washed them as well as he could.

Slocum left the lamp on the ground and upended the bench, wedging it against the door and making sure the other end was dug into the dirt. He tested the door and found it solid. Finally he let out a deep sigh and sat down on the bunk.

Merry Atwood drew away from him, huddling in the corner with her knees still sharply up in front of her. She stared at him, saying nothing.

Slocum had been ready to be angry with her, to blame her for not trusting him back at the Gem. He had thought he would say something about getting knocked over the head and having the dead man's wallet stolen from his pocket. But now that he looked at the girl he knew two things. The first was that a lot of that anger was for his own mistakes. The second thing was that the girl had already suffered far more than she deserved, and partly because—or so he guessed—she had taken a chance on leaving the stage station to go back and do the right thing— to return the wallet. He didn't say anything for a moment, and in that moment the anger disappeared.

"It must have been rough," he said gently.

The girl's numb expression suddenly dissolved in tears. She could hold herself in, perhaps, as a defense against the brutality, but there was no defense against the slightest show of sympathy. She cried uncontrollably, and Slocum reached to touch her, but she jerked away. Slocum sat back and let her cry a minute or two, then took her hand. It was stiff in his, but she didn't pull it back. He just held it without pressure. After another minute her fingers started to tighten about his. Her crying was losing its force. Part of the blanket had started to fall away from her shoulders, and he pulled it up around her with his free hand. She gripped that one, too, trapping it against her shoulder, and leaned forward to bury her head in the hollow of his neck. He felt her warmth, and he felt the heat of his own stirring deep within. He had never wanted her more than at that moment, and he trembled slightly with the effort of resisting. "I didn't know," she said again, and he could feel her breath against his neck.

"I understand," said Slocum.

"I thought you were—" Suddenly he could feel her body stiffen. She pulled away again, withdrawing into the corner against the rough logs. "How come you're here?" she said.

"Three reasons. None of them is because I'm a thief."

The girl's eyes were harder, as if she had found new strength after the tears. "That's what *they* seem to think."

"That's what I wanted them to think, Merry."

She was studying his face, and he met her eyes, letting her see whatever there was to see. "Those men aren't stupid," she finally said.

"True enough. And I can't claim I've always been on the right side of the law, either."

She thought about that, and then the suspicion seemed to leave her eyes. "I don't know," she said in a small, tired voice. "I'm too whipped to fight anymore. You said there were three reasons?"

Slocum went back to the beginning and told her the story in hushed tones, glancing occasionally toward the door. He told her about the soap salesman and the dead pilgrim from Philadelphia; the first meeting with Swearingen; the incident with the stage and the promise to Horatio Brown; the escape at the station house; the talk with Warren Bates and the second visit to the Gem Saloon; and his method of joining the gang at robbers' roost. Merry nodded occasionally, putting in a word here and there to confirm the things he'd guessed at.

"You're right," she finally said. "As soon as I heard about you from Mr. Bates I understood how you'd acquired the wallet. It upset me terribly that I'd been so unfair to you."

"Think how I must have felt." Slocum said it with a grin.

Merry showed him a fleeting smile. "Anyway, I decided to try to return it to you and set you free. And . . . apologize."

"That's when they caught you?"

She nodded. "Just as I was turning up the alley."

"That took guts, Merry. I admire what you did."

"It just seemed right."

Slocum took her hand and squeezed it hard. This was the kind of girl he should have met a long time ago. "So Swearingen still has the rest of the cash?"

"What cash?"

"The thousand dollars."

Merry was staring at him with a blank look.

"Remember when you counted it?" Slocum said. "You mentioned that there was a thousand three hundred thirty-two dollars in the wallet. When I got it from Swearingen's safe, there was only three hundred and five dollars. Take out the price of the ticket you bought, and that still leaves a thousand dollars missing."

"And you don't know what became of it?"

Slocum shook his head. "Swearingen claimed he never touched it. Was he lying?"

"I'm afraid I can't help you there, Mr. Slocum."

"You mean he was?"

Merry was frowning, and now she looked away. "I mean I just . . . can't help you."

Slocum stared at Merry, remembering the identification cards missing from the wallet. An idea was already forming in his mind. He was about to ask her another question when he heard a faint brush of footsteps outside. A second later there was a loud knock on the door.

"What's the matter, Lacey?" said Quince's voice. "Can't you get it up? Come on out and give a real man a chance."

Merry gripped Slocum's shoulder. "Don't leave me," she pleaded. "He's the worst of them all."

Slocum chewed at his lower lip a moment. "I guess I'll keep trying till I get it right," he called through the door. "Just might take all night."

"Hey!" said Quince, and Slocum saw that he was trying to open the door. Slocum pulled the thong off the hammer of his Colt and aimed carefully, placing his shot about a foot over where Quince's head would have to be.

"Now that was a warning," Slocum yelled, deafened slightly by the explosion in the little room. "The next man that tries that door will wind up dead."

"Who the hell do you think you are?" Quince complained.

"I thought I just told you, asshole. I'm the man that's gonna kill anyone who disturbs me."

Slocum heard the murmur of other voices approaching and Merry tightened the grip of her fingers on his arm.

"Now what's going on here?" said Chambers' voice.

They heard Quince complaining to his boss, and then Chambers said, "Lacey, I got to ask you to come outa there."

"I guess not," said Slocum.

"That's an order, boy."

"Sorry."

"You sure are tryin' hard to make enemies around here."

"Some things can't be helped."

"Is she worth all the trouble, Lacey?"

Slocum glanced at Merry Atwood's worried face and gave her a wink. "Won't be no trouble unless you try coming through that door."

The bandits outside fell to talking among themselves, and Slocum heard Quince and a couple of others arguing for a direct assault on the cabin. But Chambers was obviously worried about the effect of a shooting match on the size of his gang, and finally he put down the last notes of dissent.

"You got till mornin'," he called to Slocum.

"I oughta be done by then, Chambers."

"You better be havin' a damn good time, though, 'cause you're gonna pay for it. Hear me? Come mornin', you're gonna answer to me."

With that Chambers led the other men away. Their voices faded slowly, and in a few seconds he heard the door of the other cabin opening and closing.

Merry didn't loosen her grip on Slocum's arm. "What will they do?" she whispered.

Slocum shrugged. "Nothing fatal. He'll try to tame me somehow. Show me who's the boss."

"Like a fight, you mean?"

Slocum shrugged once more. "If he's even a bit fair-minded. If I'm not so lucky it could be something like a whipping."

"I'm sorry, John, I never meant for you to go through that. I've been nothing but trouble to you ever since—"

Slocum stopped her with his fingers to her lips. "I already told you not to worry. It's been mixed up from the beginning, and it's no one's fault—except maybe Swearingen's. I been whipped before, and even beaten once or twice. I still get up."

"But I feel so—"

"I know. Try to fight it. The only thing we should be worrying about right now is getting the hell out of here before Parker comes back."

"Parker?"

"A member of the gang, apparently. Were there seven men here altogether?"

"I think so." Merry lowered her eyes. "I'm afraid . . . I guess I lost track."

Slocum bit the inside of his lip. "Anyway, someone named Parker went into Deadwood for supplies. He's due back tomorrow."

Merry looked perplexed.

"If he goes anywhere near the Gem . . ." Slocum began.

Merry's eyes went wide. "He'll hear about what happened!"

Slocum nodded. "There can't be all that many of us around with black hair and green eyes. Not to mention the coincidence of Lacey showing up just when Slocum disappears."

"What about Horatio Brown?"

"He'll have to make do with what I have. If I wind up dead he won't have anything at all."

Merry's eyes were glistening with tears. "Damn it, John, none of this would have happened if I hadn't—"

"What?" snapped Slocum. "Tried to save your life the best way you knew how? I think that's what you said, isn't it?"

"But I had no right—"

"Listen." He took her shoulders and gave them a little shake. "You did what you thought you had to do, partly because I didn't give you much reason to hope. Now you feel bad, and I appreciate that, but we all wind up doing things we wish we hadn't. It's time to stop looking back."

"I'll try," she said, with a tentative smile.

"Good."

"I don't know how I can ever repay you, though." She looked down at herself and then back into Slocum's eyes. "I'd offer you . . . I mean, I wish I could . . ."

"Forget it," said Slocum. "This isn't the time or place."

"Maybe later . . ."

"Yeah. Maybe."

She laid her head on his shoulder again, and for a while

there was only an occasional sputtering from the oil lamp and the flutter of mice scampering over the roof. Then the girl raised her head again. Her voice was quiet and composed.

"What are we going to do?" she said.

"That's a good question."

"Really, John."

"Okay. I don't see trying to get out of here tonight, to begin with. They might be watching the cabin, and even if they aren't they're sittin' on most of my gear. We'd also have a hell of a time getting at the horses—and a hell of a time getting up that mountain without horses."

"But you said that man—Parker—was coming back tomorrow."

Slocum nodded. "I see only one way out," he said, and when he finished telling her about it she sighed and said, "I sure hope it works."

They were silent a few more minutes, and then Merry looked at him from beneath her eyelashes. "It'll be cold tonight."

"Yeah."

"There's only the two blankets."

"I got my coat."

"No. We can keep each other warm."

"You sure, Merry?"

She nodded. "I think it might . . . be good for me."

23

Slocum didn't know what time it was that he awoke. He looked quickly at the door, but there was no gray light at the cracks. He held his breath a moment, but he heard no sound. He had left the oil lamp burning, the wick trimmed as low as possible, so he could see what he was doing if the bandits tried to rush the cabin. Now he turned to look at the girl lying beside him in the soft glow of the light and found her watching him. Their faces were only a few inches apart.

"Hi," she whispered.

Slocum smiled. "Have you slept?"

"A little. I was thinking about home."

"You'll be there soon enough."

The girl frowned. "That's just it, John. I'm not sure I can anymore." She looked away, and then back into his eyes with a new intensity. "I'm not sure I want to."

"Ah." Slocum was quiet a moment, guessing at some of Merry's thoughts. "No one says you have to go back," he finally told her. "There's a lot of room here. A lot of opportunity. Places you can lose yourself, if you want."

"John?" She pressed her lips together for a moment. "John, what do you think you'll do after all this?"

"Same as I've always done, I guess. Go somewhere else." Slocum saw sadness in the girl's eyes before she lowered them, and he realized he wasn't exactly feeling cheerful himself. "You had me pegged that first night in the Gem," he said. "Remember? You said I'd eventually move on because that was the type of man I was."

"People change, sometimes."

"Sometimes."

He still couldn't see Merry's eyes. "Is it me?" she said. "Is it because of all the . . . all the men?"

"No!" Slocum instinctively put his arms around the girl. "Don't you even begin to think that way."

"Really?"

"It's driving me crazy, wishing I could tell you lies tonight, just so we could have some time together."

"Really, John?"

Slocum looked at her and waited for her eyes to meet his again. Their lips came together, and they kissed, and then they lay together for a time. The flickering lamplight cast dancing shadows across the rough ceiling.

Slocum slowly became aware of Merry's breathing. It was a little shallower, he thought, a little hotter against his neck. Suddenly she reached around back for his hand and placed it against her throat. "Please," she whispered. "Softly." She was moving his hand back and forth, but she held it so that he was just barely touching her skin. After a moment she took her own hand away. Her eyes were still closed.

Slocum didn't stop. He touched her neck and shoulders. Brushed her hair away from one ear and kissed it. His hand moved slowly down and lightly touched one breast. She flinched, but relaxed immediately and breathed more deeply. He cupped the full breast in his hand and touched it with his lips. He kissed the nipple, letting his hand work slowly down across her soft belly. His fingers came to the tight curls of hair betwen her legs, hesitating an instant before exploring for the small hardness hidden there in the wet folds of flesh. He found it, rolled it beneath his finger, and heard a gasp in his ear. It was followed by a rush of hot breath.

"How do you know?" she gasped.

"I aim to please, ma'am."

Slocum slipped his fingers deep inside her, and she began to writhe beneath his hand. His thumb remained outside, moving over the hard swollen tissue in a way that made Merry shudder.

"That's *perfect*," she said. "You're a master!"

Slocum kissed her breasts and moved his fingers, holding her shoulders in the arm beneath him.

"Go ahead," she said. Her voice was dry and hoarse, but urgent. "Go *ahead*, John!"

He hesitated a moment longer. She put her lips next to his ear. "Fuck me, damn it."

Slocum rolled over onto her, and she guided him in with hungry hands. He moved between her legs, and almost immediately she was crying out, her fingers digging into his back. Slowly she subsided, gasping, sweat gleaming on her face.

"You're a beautiful woman," Slocum whispered in her ear. "Ain't many like you."

She lay beneath him, clinging to him, and he was still hard inside her. He looked down and saw tears brimming over her eyelids. He leaned on an elbow and brushed them away. And after a minute or two he felt her hips begin to squirm beneath him. Her eyes widened when he grinned at her.

"Oh God," she said. "Again?"

Slocum only winked, resuming the slow rhythm. She said his name once, and then again, still clinging to him. The climax was much longer coming this time, but her cries were also wilder, and this time he also allowed himself to join her. The hunger for her had built steadily since the first conversation, and now the feeling of release seemed to thunder through his body and roar in his ears. They lay together for a long time, fully drained and unmoving. At some point they slept. But just before he slept, a weary smile came to Slocum's lips. He remembered wondering if Merry's cries had awakened the outlaws next door, and he murmured to himself, *What do you think of that, you bastards?*

Then he remembered nothing more.

24

"Lacey!"

Slocum came awake with a start. He shook his head to clear it and felt the girl's hand gripping his shoulder.

"Goddamn it, Lacey, get your ass out here."

It was Bill Chambers' voice, Slocum decided.

"Hang on," he hollered. "I'm on my way."

"It doesn't sound promising," Merry whispered in his ear.

"Don't worry. The more intent they are on me, the better."

He finished with the buttons on his shirt and reached for his trousers. When he was strapping on the gunbelt Merry handed him his coat. It was heavy with the weight of Al Swearingen's Smith and Wesson revolvers. He slipped into the coat and pulled the girl into the far corner of the room. He checked the shells in one of the Smiths and worked the action a couple of times before he pressed the gun in Merry's hand.

"It's easy to use," he said. "Just cock it—like this—just point it in the general direction, and pull the trigger."

"Lacey!"

Slocum turned his head to yell. "Hold your goddamn water." Then in a near-whisper: "The trigger will be hard to pull. Just hold your breath and do your best. Can you manage?"

The girl nodded.

"You won't want to do it. It's not natural to kill. But if you have to, just think of these last few days."

He saw the chill come into her eyes, the compression of her lips, and the clenching of the muscles in her jaw.

"That's right," he said. "Just keep thinking about what'll happen if you don't pull the trigger."

The girl nodded again.

"Just one thing, Merry." Slocum smiled. "Make sure it isn't me on the other end."

Merry looked more frightened than amused. She put a hand on his arm. It was trembling slightly. "Be careful," she begged. "Please be careful."

Slocum's smile turned to a grin. "Don't worry. You're the only one who's ever managed to knock me out with my own gun." He stepped back for a better view of her body. "And besides, I got something to look forward to."

Merry blushed and lowered her eyes.

"Now stay here," said Slocum, and left her in the corner while he crossed to the door and unjammed the bench. He took one last look at the girl, winked at her as he slipped the thong off the hammer of his Colt, and threw the door open.

Chambers and the other five men were ranged around the front of the cabin, standing about twenty feet off. No one had their guns out. Chambers looked angry, but the one named Quince was smiling. As soon as he guessed what was about to happen Slocum stepped off the porch and started walking toward the other cabin, moving up the bank of the little stream, away from the front of the place where he'd spent the night.

"You boys look all set for bear," Slocum said lightly.

"And you're the bear," said Quince.

Slocum kept walking. The bandits moved along beside him, angling closer. "You got a lesson to learn," Chambers explained. "Now I liked you well enough, damnit, but you can't go buckin' the crowd like this."

"Says who?"

"Me," said Quince.

Slocum looked at him. "You?"

Quince looked at Chambers, who said, "I told him he could take you on, Lacey. An' if he don't do the job—then I will."

Slocum was still walking. He stopped near the far corner of the next cabin and studied Quince, who was a couple of inches shorter than Slocum and had a wiry frame. Slocum shook his head.

"Well, if you want to send a boy to do a man's work"— he was slipping out of his coat—"might as well get it over with."

Slocum dropped his coat on the ground, the gunbelt on top of it, and moved around the side of the cabin as if to make room for himself to maneuver in. The other men circled around. As Quince began closing in, Slocum chanced a quick look over his shoulder. When he saw that the main cabin now blocked any view of Merry's door, he turned his attention back to Quince.

At first it looked as if the outlaw was still smiling, but Slocum saw that his face was formed around a contorted grin. He heard the harsh rasp of breath through Quince's teeth. And when the man lashed out with a fast hook, Slocum understood that he was somehow a little off-balance in the head. Slocum swallowed hard, wishing he hadn't given up his gun so easily. A man like Quince could be dangerously unpredicatble.

At that instant the outlaw charged. He and Slocum had been circling each other like boxers, but now the bandit came on with a series of wild punches. Not all that effective, but they were so fast that Slocum had trouble staying out of their way. There was a puzzled frown on his face as he brought his elbow down hard on Quince's skull.

Quince cried out and crumpled in the dirt, holding his head with both hands. Slocum cursed himself. It was important to make this fight last. He noticed that Chambers and the other four bandits all had their eyes on Quince, waiting to see what he would do. The answer caught Slocum by surprise.

Instead of coming slowly out of it, and then getting on with the wary footwork of circling his opponent, Quince was suddenly up and fighting. One instant he was moaning on the ground, the next he was up and pounding Slocum with his fists. A blow to the temple, another to the chin, a wild punch that landed on the shoulder. Slocum stumbled back to the sudden sound of encouraging yells from the bandits. They were cheering Quince's recovery. Slocum fought back, but his own fists had trouble finding their mark. The wiry Quince was all over Slocum, moving frantically and never letting up. It was impossible to guess where he might be from one split second to the next.

Confused, Slocum retreated another foot or two toward open ground—until he saw the hillside beyond Merry's cabin coming into view. He wasn't sure whether it was his eyesight or his imagination that caught a glimpse of movement there, but he didn't stop to look. He suddenly moved inside Quince's flailing arms and landed two solid blows to his belly. They didn't seem to have an effect. Slocum backed up again, this time toward the wall of the bandit's cabin, and when he got a good look at Quince's face the fear gripped him again. The man's eyes bulged from their sockets, and there was a touch of white foam at his mouth. Slocum found himself wondering if anything would stop this man, short of a bullet. If even *that* would do it. Then he tried to shrug off the foolish superstitions.

Slocum didn't have any more time to think. Quince kept coming at him, relentless, raining blows in every direction. He tried to kick Slocum between the legs, and that was coming too close to home for Slocum's comfort. He decided it was time to stop fooling around. For the second time he moved directly into the flailing arms, dimly aware of the yells from the bandits, and landed two more blows in Quince's stomach. His fists sank deep.

This time the bandit blew out a lungful of air and backed off an instant. Slocum stayed on him, driving a fist home above the man's heart and another one on his jaw just in front of his ear. Still the man tried to keep coming, but he had lost the drive. His blows were weaker, and now it was Slocum who was relentless. He blackened Quince's eye. He turned him on his heel with a wide roundhouse. And then he jumped off to one side and struck at his kidney. Quince was reeling. The other bandits were yelling louder than ever, but already with the bitter disappointment of defeat. Slocum waited for the man's guard to drop a little more, and then he gathered all his strength, bringing his fist up from somewhere near the ground, for a final blow on the point of Quince's jaw. The bandit staggered, then fell to the ground and lay still.

For a moment there was only the sound of Slocum's gasping breath as he worked to fill his lungs. He was looking at Chambers, who had his eyes on Quince. Chambers shook his head and sighed. "Well, he wanted to try. Couldn't very well have said no." Then Chambers looked up at Slocum. "You willin' to share with your friends now?"

"I guess not," Slocum said levelly.

Chambers shook his head again, rolling his massive shoulders as he clenched and unclenched his fists. "I was hopin' it wouldn't come to this," he said.

Slocum grinned, leaning forward on the balls of his feet. "Me too, Bill."

"Wait a minute!"

It was one of the bandits, shading his eyes and looking up the hill over the roof of the cabin. The others looked too, as did Slocum, although he was edging toward his coat and gun.

"What the fuck's she trying to pull?" said another of the bandits.

"Why that little bitch," said Chambers. Suddenly he frowned and started to turn. Slocum saw him and dove for the gun. The other bandits hadn't formed suspicions—didn't know what was going on. They saw Slocum diving and rolling and saw their boss slapping his holster, but they didn't know why, so they were slow to react. Slocum stopped rolling with his gun free and trained on Chambers. The outlaw leader's hand was on the butt of his pistol and still moving.

"No!" Slocum yelled. In the same instant it took to yell the word, Chambers' gun was already out of his holster. Slocum's brain registered that the man was fast, that any hesitation now would be fatal, and his instinct took over. When Chambers' arm was half raised, Slocum fired a slug into the man's chest. His thumb instantly found the hammer, and he cocked and fired again. Chambers' arm kept coming up, and he fired once, the bullet puffing into the dirt half a foot to the right of Slocum's shoulder. Then the big man's arm dropped, and his body was already turning from the impact of the bullets. Chambers staggered back. He started to raise his gun again, slowly. Slocum waited, thankful when he didn't have to waste another bullet.

All this happened almost literally in the blink of an eye. The other bandits saw their boss drawing, heard Slocum shout, and heard three shots that came together so fast they sounded almost as one. And before they knew what to do they found themselves facing Slocum's Colt, the hammer already drawn back. They stared at him, and finally one of them began to understand.

"Hey," he said, and nodded toward the hillside. "D'you have anything to do with that?"

"Shut up," Slocum barked. He was deliberately harsh, hoping to tame the outlaws and dominate the situation with the force of his personality. Quince was just now stirring, and that would make five men against one. The chances were that he could pick them off, or scare them out of trying anything. But he only had four shots left, and they knew that. And if they ever tried to make a move all together, it would get a little uncomfortable. That was why he'd hoped to get Merry safely on the ridge, and then find some pretext to get away from the camp.

Slocum was carefully getting to his feet when a shot echoed down from the hill. A second later there was another shot followed instantly by a third. The outlaws turned their heads toward the sound—except the one who looked the craftiest, who kept his eyes on Slocum, which might have helped Slocum fight the urge to do the same. Instead he ordered the bandits to turn around and walk toward the cabin. They hesitated, measuring him and eyeing his gun, none of them wanting to be the first to obey.

Slocum's tone turned fierce. *"Move,* you assholes."

They all moved together, reluctantly, shuffling toward the door of the cabin. They held their hands slightly away from their sides, more as protection for themselves than anything—to make sure the edgy green-eyed bastard didn't make a mistake and shoot one of them in the back.

Slocum scooped up his coat and followed. "You're doin' fine," he said. "Just keep acting sensible and you'll all live to steal more horses."

They came to the door, and Slocum ordered them to stop. The little cloud of dust they'd been kicking up now drifted away in the morning breeze. Slocum ached to know what had happened on the hill. He thought of the returning Parker. He listened, but there were no sounds of an approaching horse.

Now the tricky part.

"Listen to me," Slocum said after a moment. "You're all gonna go through that door together, crowding each other like a mob. Arm to arm. I see you startin' to break up and I'll get nervous and get to shooting. You won't be able to afford it, bunched up like that. Right?"

There was a bit of murmuring from the bandits.

"Right! And you're gonna stop when you're halfway through that door. One of you will get my warbag and bedroll and toss it over their heads. I see anything besides my warbag or bedroll... well, I don't have to spell it out, do I?"

No answer. Slocum laid his coat on the ground and bent to fish Swearingen's second Smith and Wesson from the pocket.

"Look at me," said Slocum.

The five faces turned toward him and saw that he had both hands filled. They'd have to assume he could get both guns firing at the same time, which he could if he had to.

"Now *do* it!"

The faces stayed turned toward him a moment longer—the little gesture of defiance that men use to keep one last grip on their pride. Then they moved in a compact bunch toward the cabin. It didn't look as if they would stop in the doorway. Slocum called out a harsh order and the mass halted. Their broad backs filled the opening. After a second he saw his gear come sailing over their shoulders, thrown harder than necessary so that it landed with some force quite a distance away. He saw the men start to move again, but another command stopped them while he retrieved his saddle from against the front wall. The Henry was still in its scabbard. He holstered his Colt and quickly jacked a shell into the rifle's chamber.

"We're almost done," Slocum called out. "The last thing you have to understand is how foolish it would be to stick your nose out of that cabin. I'll kill you, and that's a promise. Now get the fuck inside and shut the door, and keep thinking about the effective range of this Henry."

Slocum tensely watched the men shuffle inside, waiting for a flash of movement from the deep shadows beyond. When he saw the door swing closed he was flooded with a sudden sense of relief, a surge of something like wild joy.

Slocum gathered his warbag and bedroll and tied them down, using the leather thongs anchored to his saddle, all the time keeping his eyes on the cabin. He was about to hoist the saddle when he saw a vertical line of shadow that told him the door was being slowly opened. Instantly he threw the Henry to his shoulder and placed a shot through the middle of the door. It closed. He kept the carbine in his right hand, using his left to throw the loaded saddle over his shoulder.

Slocum backed carefully toward the far side of the bowl, where his little spotted pony was grazing. It watched him as he came. Slocum was watching the cabin, and trying to sneak an occasional glance up the hill. The sense of joy—that physical release of mere survival—was already starting to fade as he thought about Merry Atwood. He could see nothing of the girl, but he also saw nothing of any other riders up there. He had told Merry to wait along the limestone ledge that formed one side of the bowl, just where it met the grassy slope to the east. He had remembered a small stand of pines there, and that's where he hoped he'd find her.

First he had to get there. He'd almost reached the horse when he started to get nervous, knowing that the Henry wouldn't be as effective now, at about eighty yards, especially with snap shots off the shoulder. He was beginning to wonder what kind of chances the outlaws might take when the door to the cabin was thrown open and the bandits started pouring out, scattering to each side.

Slocum took his first shot from the hip, even while he was dropping the saddle, then levered another round into the chamber and took a bead. He fired and a man went down, clutching his leg. Slocum levered, fired again. Another of the bandits spun back into the logs and slumped toward the ground. Slocum saw that the outlaws were trying to slip around the side of the cabin to find cover. He worried less about accuracy and cranked the lever as fast as he could to pour lead on all sides. The bandits had seen two men go down in the first seconds, and now they felt the slugs ripping by everywhere. Quince felt a burn along his neck. It was enough to stop his momentum, and he retreated to the cabin door, followed by the two bandits still standing. The one gripping his leg was writhing in the dirt, moaning with pain. The one against the logs didn't move at all.

Slocum stared grimly at the cabin and then knelt down to fish blindly in the warbag, eyes still fixed on the cabin door.

He figured they were watching him, and he wanted to make sure they knew what the odds were. He found the shells for his Henry and slowly, with deliberate calm, reloaded the rifle.

The firing had driven his horse farther away, right up to the edge of the slope that rimmed the bowl. Slocum moved more quickly now, still watching the door but hoping the outlaws would take a little time getting their courage back. If they were smarter they would have known that this was the best time to strike, but if they were smarter they wouldn't likely be trying to steal livestock for a living.

It took a minute or two to get close to the nervous pony, and another minute to get the bit between her teeth and the saddle on her back. Slocum jerked the cinch tight and vaulted lightly into the saddle, Henry still in his hand, and with a wild yell he began to scatter the other horses. It was more a gesture than anything. He fired a couple of shots and made two quick passes at the little herd, but they only scrambled a few yards up the hill before they felt safe enough to stop and watch. Figuring the distance to the cabin and the time to saddle up and get organized, Slocum decided he'd given himself about five minutes' head start.

On the last pass at the outlaw remuda he kept running his pony up the side of the hill, toward the corner where the slope met the limestone cap rock.

There was still no sign of Merry.

25

Slocum had some second thoughts when he was halfway up the hill. He changed course and sent his pony almost straight up the slope. The little mountain-bred horse took the steeper angle in stride, Slocum leaning far forward in the saddle to keep his balance. He almost had to stand in the stirrups. But the spotted pony lunged gamely up the hill, propelling itself on its wiry legs of rugged muscle. The horse grunted with each new thrust and was breathing hard inside of a few seconds, but it kept going. Slocum shook his head in admiration, murmuring encouragement. The ridge line and the trees were only a few yards away.

Slocum heard the boom of rifles from the bottom of the bowl. Slugs started plunking into the hillside. He didn't bother to look back. Not much he could do about it, and he was almost a quarter mile away by now. He pulled up for a second in the cover of the trees to take a look. Three men were carrying rifles and saddles toward their horses. The men were trying to run, the cinches and stirrups flapping madly behind them. Slocum grinned at the sight. He also nodded in satisfaction when he saw that the fourth outlaw was holding his leg, just watching the others go, while the one that was slumped against the cabin hadn't moved at all. Slocum hadn't planned it that way, but it looked like the odds were getting better every minute.

Except that he didn't have the time to be cautious anymore. Slocum had changed direction on the hillside because he didn't want to go straight toward the meeting place by the limestone ledge. He remembered the two shots coming so close together up there, which meant that whoever Merry encountered must have fired at least one of them—if not the first shot. Slocum had no way of knowing what he'd find. He had decided to at least avoid the most obvious ambush possibility.

Now he couldn't afford any further scouting. He exchanged the Henry for his Colt and ran his horse through the pines, dodging the low branches of an occasional burr oak. He went straight at the junction of the cap rock and the grassy hillside. He had his gun up, and his unfocused eyes were alert for the first sign of movement. It was a relief to hear Merry's voice.

"Over here, John!"

Slocum saw her sagging against the rock face, the Smith and Wesson dangling from her hand. She seemed to be staring past him, her eyes looking a little wild. The body of a man was lying face down just a few feet to the right of the girl. Slocum stopped his horse over the body and jumped off. There was a gun in the man's hand. Slocum stepped on the gun and then leaned down to pick it up. Only then did he turn the body over with a toe of his boot, standing between it and Merry to act as a bit of a shield.

The man had taken a bullet low in the belly. His free hand was still clutching the hole, and his face was frozen in a grimace of agony. Slocum turned him over again.

"Thank you," said the girl.

Slocum turned and saw her staring.

"It was horrible," she said. Her voice trembled, and she seemed to be talking more to herself than to Slocum. "I knew I had to do something. He was the one they called Parker. I *had* to shoot. But it was horrible to watch him die."

"I know, Merry. It never gets any easier. He didn't hit you with anything?"

She shook her head. "I don't think he believed I'd fire." Her eyes came up to Slocum's face with a pleading look. "I *told* him I would. I told him to put the gun down, but he laughed. He got off his horse and started coming toward me."

"You had no choice, Merry." Slocum wrapped her in his arms. "You couldn't have done anything different. You just had no choice."

"I told him not to come any closer, but he just laughed." Her voice faded a moment, and she gripped him tightly. "I *had* to shoot, John."

"I know. You had to."

"He seemed real surprised."

"I'll bet."

"He looked down at himself, to make sure he wasn't hit, I guess. Then he cursed me and started to raise his gun again."

"You both shot at the same time?"

She nodded. "I guess that's when I hit him. He turned around a little and held himself like . . . like that. Then he started . . . he was down . . ."

"Stop thinking about it, Merry."

"I can't."

Slocum took a quick glance over his shoulder. Nothing coming yet, but they'd be saddling the horses by now. "Was that fellow riding?" he asked.

Merry nodded.

"Where'd the horse go?"

The girl lifted her chin in the direction of the trees.

"Can't be too far," Slocum murmured. Then he made a decision and scooped Merry up in his arms and onto his saddle. He jumped on behind her, kicking his horse on into the forest with one more look back. So far the bandits hadn't made it to the top of the hill.

Slocum found a young gelding not far away, its reins tangled in a fallen limb. He rode up alongside and flipped open the pouches behind the saddle, making a sound of satisfaction when he found a bottle of whiskey there. He uncapped it and handed it to the girl. She obediently took a swallow, and made a face.

"Can you ride?" Slocum asked. "I mean, can you run full out? We'll go a lot farther on two horses."

The girl took a deep breath, a little life coming back into her eyes. "I can try," she said. "Just keep an eye on me."

"You don't have to tell me to do that."

Merry turned to look at Slocum and saw his grin. "Oh, you," she said, her eyes twinkling a little. "I thought this was serious."

Slocum let his grin disappear. "Yeah, I'm afraid it is. They can't be more than a couple of minutes behind us." He slipped his hand down into his warbag and came out with his spare Navy. It was fully loaded, and so it went into his holster. The other one he stuffed into his belt.

Merry suddenly looked down at Swearingen's revolver, forgotten in her hand. "What about this?" she said.

"Might as well hang on to it."

"I won't be much help. I missed the first time."

"You did all right. Just remember that two people shooting will keep 'em ducking. It'll help spoil their aim."

Merry shuddered. "I hope they don't get that close."

"Yeah," Slocum agreed again. He lifted Merry sideways into the other saddle and then leaned over to untangle the reins, passing them up to put in the girl's hands.

"Just grab on tight and keep ticklin' his ribs," Slocum said grimly. "We've still got a ways to go and some hard riding to do before we get there."

The girl gave him a look of resignation, raising her eyebrows and shrugging her shoulders as if to say, *What else is new?* Out loud she said, "Anytime."

Slocum could hear them now, a distant thundering and shuddering pound of hooves in the hard-packed dirt of the hillside, the slap of leather, the snorts of the bandits' ponies, the war cries of the bandits themselves. He knew the sounds of his own retreat would be covered, but he also knew the outlaws would be coming upon the body of their partner within a minute. He slapped the rump of Merry's horse and ran along beside her through the trees, pointing south for the trail back to the Chambers brothers' stage station—and away from Deadwood.

It was the only sure route Slocum knew of through the maze of Black Hills canyons, but he had no intention of staying with it. This first move would be a feint. He hoped to make it seem as if he was heading in the obvious direction, so they wouldn't slow down to read his trail. If they headed for the stage road at a dead run, they might miss the spot where Slocum cut off to the side to get out of their way.

The horses raced through the trees in a wild, lurching gait. Slocum looked back to see Merry crouched low with her arms around the neck of her gelding, her eyes popped wide with fear. Behind her there was no sight of anything else. He hoped the bandits couldn't hear them. After another mile he eased up a bit to save the horses. He caught Merry's eye and flashed her a reassuring smile.

They came to the meadow where he'd seen the antelope the day before. As they galloped into the open, Slocum eased his Colt from the holster. They swooped down the little ravine and started up the broad slope on the other side. Slocum looked behind and saw the clods of grass and dirt being thrown up by the laboring horses. He saw the fresh cuts in the meadow, as easy to follow as any road. he pointed with the Colt to show Merry where they should enter the trees again. When they were almost there he looked back. Still no sight of hte outlaws. An odd thought struck him: that it must be a comfort to be a believer, so you could pray. All he could do was trust in his own instincts. Then it occured to him he hadn't done all that badly iln the job of staying alive.

He didn't look back again until he and Merry had ridden well into the trees, and then he held out his hand, slowing to a walk. From the deep shadow of the pines he gazed between the tall tree trunks. But again he heard the outlaws before he saw them, heard their horses and heard the outlaws' shouts. He had already turned back north, on a course parallel with the tree line. Now he held to a brisk trot while he watched the pursuers pull up for a second at the edge of the meadow, holding their ears to the breeze and squinting into the sunlight. They probably saw no danger of ambush. One man pointed toward the ground with a shout that carried across the meadow, and then all three men were running their horses down Slocum's trail.

Slocum allowed himself a tight smile. He knew the trail would fade and disappear among the thick matting of dead pine needles, where he'd slowed the horses, and he had no reason to think any of the three outlaws would outguess him. They would assume that in his fear of them—what else could they believe?—he'd be able to think of nothing but to run as fast as he could in a straight line.

At least for now.

Slocum tracked the outlaws with his ears. He heard them

come into the trees and go crashing by just over a slight rise, out of sight, and he heard their sounds fade slowly in the direction of the stage stop.

Now Slocum frowned. The drawback to his strategy was that Gerry Chambers would soon know all about his brother's death and the abrupt departure of Slocum and the girl. There was a good chance Chambers would disappear, and Slocum saw the same fate for his two-thousand-dollar reward. There was also a good chance that Chambers would alert Al Swearingen. If that happened then it wouldn't be long before the two of them realized that the man Chambers knew as Lacey was the same man Swearingen knew as John Slocum. He didn't know what they'd make of that—except that it would probably be a hell of a lot harder getting into Deadwood tonight.

Slocum was still glancing over his shoulder, out of habit, and now he noticed Merry staring at him with a strange expression in her eyes. He realized that he had told her nothing of his thoughts, that she had no idea what the future would hold. He stopped his horse broadside, and she pulled up on her reins, still staring at him.

"I'm thinking we've made it," Slocum said. "For now. If they don't wise up—and probably even if they do—it'll be a long time before they're able to track us down."

The girl didn't say anything.

"Well. I just thought you'd like to know." Slocum started to turn his horse, but Merry grabbed his arm. "Yes?" he said.

She opened her mouth and took a breath. She shook her head, and Slocum noticed the wet shine of her eyes. "I just...don't know how to thank you," she finally said. "Or how to tell you how bad I feel about—"

"Oh that," said Slocum. "I thought we'd already—"

"But I was such a fool! I see how good you've been, how capable, and I see I should have trusted you a long time ago. I should have *known*, somehow."

Slocum winked at her and smiled. "That's what I was tryin' to tell you at the time."

The girl laughed, and almost choked on her tears. "I know," she said, and laughed again, "I mean *next* time I'll know." Suddenly she moved her horse in closer and threw her arms around Slocum's neck. She was kissing him when a rifle cracked nearby. He felt her body stiffen and then begin to sag. Their eyes met, only inches apart. He watched hers close. Slowly. She was dead weight in his arms.

26

The girl's head flopped nervelessly to the side, and Slocum saw the shooter standing behind a tree fifty yards away. It was the bandit he'd hit in the leg. The man held a rifle just a few inches below his chin, and he was staring, apparently startled at having shot a woman. But he recovered immediately, throwing the rifle to his shoulder. Slocum was already pushing out of the saddle, his arms still wrapped around the girl. The rifle cracked again, and Slocum felt the breeze of the bullet on his cheek as he and Merry began falling between their horses. They hit the ground, and the outlaw fired a third shot.

Slocum covered the girl with his body as he snapped off a round from his Colt. It was answered by the rifle, and in that instant Slocum was up and running. He had as long as it takes to lever another round into the chamber. He stopped behind a tree trunk, and felt it shudder with the impact of a heavy slug. He looked back at Merry's body, trying to detect any sign that she was breathing. All he saw was the blood soaking her hair.

In his mind Slocum had a picture of the bandit waiting, his rifle barrel resting against the tree. He'd know within a few inches—to the left or right of that tree—where Slocum had to appear. The odds were all with the outlaw at this range. Not that the Colt wasn't accurate at fifty yards, it was just a little harder to line up the sights than on a rifle. Slocum used his time to think, but looking at the girl he also knew he didn't have much time. Normally he'd have used the weapon of patience. Now he had to take chances. He poked his head around the tree just an inch or two and in the same movement pulled it back.

He almost saw the muzzle flash from the rifle. The bullet

156

whistled by just as his head came to rest again behind the tree. He waited another minute then tried the same thing.

He caught sight of the outlaw and the rifle, but there was no shot this time. The outlaw was a quick learner.

Slocum gave the man a better target, but still pulled back before the slug came by to thunk in a pine tree several feet away. He waited another minute, aware of the sweat beading on his forehead and the sound of flies in the forest quiet. He hoped he'd established a bit of a pattern by now. He was letting a minute go by before he tried anything, and he wasn't shooting back just yet. It probably looked as though he was trying to waste the bandit's ammunition. At the end of a minute Slocum popped out on the opposite side to offer an even better target. Again he felt the breeze of the bullet on his face. The bastard is fast, Slocum thought.

But this time Slocum changed his pattern. He reappeared instantly, already bringing up his gun arm. The outlaw was taking his time operating the lever of his carbine, only half watching Slocum's tree. He probably wasn't all that worried about a man with a handgun. But Slocum sighted down the long barrel of his Colt and held his breath and deliberately squeezed the trigger. The shot came as a surprise, as it should. He brought his gun down from the recoil, cocking it in the same motion, and fired again. In a panic, the outlaw had just thrown the rifle to his shoulder again when the slugs caught him high on the chest. Slocum was already running toward him as he toppled backward onto the pine needles.

The man's eyes were still open, but he was dead. Blood filled his open mouth, and his boot heels drummed against the ground. He had tied a faded blue bandanna around his leg, pinching the blood-soaked trousers. Slocum stared at the dead man for a moment, then glanced up to find his horse. It was tethered farther back in the trees, with no saddle but lots of blood on the flanks. The bandit had obviously decided to follow at his own pace, and either he had heard Slocum's movements or he'd been able to do a better job of reading the trail.

Slocum shook his head. "You were too smart for your own good," he murmured. Then he turned away.

Slocum's ears were ringing a little from the shots, and he

didn't even try to listen for the rest of the gang as he ran back toward the girl. He'd just hope they hadn't heard the shots.

He knelt beside Merry, fingering the thick blond curls of her hair until he found the wound. He had already taken hope when he saw that there were no bulges in her head, no popped eyeballs like you get when a rifle slug bursts into the brain. Instead the bullet had torn loose a jagged piece of her scalp. Slocum's fingertips, greasy with blood, spread the hair to each side. He watched the skin slide with it. In the separation he could see the white sheen of her skull, and the ugly groove in her bone. Slocum nodded, but he was still worried. The blood was oozing freely from the tear and showed no sign of letting up. Merry could still bleed to death.

Chewing tensely on the inside of his lip, moving as fast as he could, Slocum prepared himself. He slipped his Henry from its scabbard and leaned it against a tree. He laid his Colts on the ground. He pulled his warbag off the saddle and dug out the bottle of whiskey provided by Parker, followed by a little pouch in which he kept a heavy needle and some thread. Normally he used it for sewing leather. Only once had he used it on himself, and never on anyone else.

Slocum opened the whiskey and splashed a little into the bleeding hole. A spasm rolled through the girl's body. Slocum almost felt the pain himself, curling his lips as he began to recap the bottle. He glanced at it and, with a shrug, put it to his lips. He allowed himself two swallows. He closed his eyes a moment. When he opened them, looking at the blood in Merry's golden hair, he sighed deeply, then began to thread his needle.

Slocum held the collar of his coat tighter around his neck as he stared down at the flickering lights of Deadwood. He was high up in the trees, and the wind was blowing here, a chilly wind. He glanced back with a worried frown at the horse he was leading, seeing that the girl had still not stirred. She was only a quiet bundle leaning forward from the saddle. Slocum had tied her feet around the horse's belly and her hands around its neck. Her body was cushioned by a wadded blanket and covered by another one.

He had pulled the flaps of skin together as best he could, then ripped up parts of Merry's gown to bandage her head. The bleeding had mostly stopped, but Merry had never come out of it. The one good sign was that she seemed to be breathing regularly. Slocum figured it was a blessing that she'd been spared the pain of the long ride and the wait for darkness, but only if she were planning to wake up sometime. He looked at the form under the blanket a long moment, and many thoughts passed through his head.

The long ride had been made even longer by the broken land of the Black Hills. He had found mountain slopes too steep to go down, rock walls that suddenly barred his way, and gaps in the walls that led to dead ends. He began to understand the frustrations of the expedition under General Custer, which came to the hills in '74. They, too, had plenty of false starts. But Slocum continued working slowly north and east, keeping one eye on his back trail, and finally managed to strike the stage road just a few miles from Deadwood without running into the outlaws again. He had holed up in the trees then, waiting for the night to cover the rest of his trip.

But as he watched the lights in the gulch, Slocum wasn't thinking about the hazards of the ride. He was thinking about Merry Atwood and the way he had felt when her body slumped in his arms. He'd been thinking about it all day. He remembered telling her the night before that he was nothing more than a drifter. He remembered the way he'd rejected any ideas she might have about him before she could say them. He was sure he'd always want to be moving on—but when it seemed that she might be dying, Slocum had felt a great hollowness in him. A bitter taste of ashes in his mouth. And all day he had considered the things he thought he wanted, and those he didn't.

He still had no answer. He looked at the quiet form once more, then touched the ribs of his horse to begin the descent into the back streets of the town. His Colts were in his belt and holster, fully charged. He gave them a light tug as he rode.

Slocum weaved his way through the dark streets, exciting nothing more than a curious look from an occasional passerby. Perhaps they saw Merry's legs sticking out beneath the blanket and perhaps they didn't, but no one seemed intent on interfering. Slocum finally found Warren Bates's small cabin and rode past it twice, looking for any sign of observation, but the shadows in the alleys and against the walls looked like nothing more than shadows. He tied the horses far back behind the cabin.

Quickly he cut the ropes holding Merry on the saddle and pulled her free. Carrying her in his arms he slipped around to the door of the cabin and tapped it with his boot. The door opened quickly, as if Bates had heard the approach. His eyes dropped to the bundle in Slocum's arms, and this time he didn't hesitate. He stepped back and opened the door wide, closing it again as soon as Slocum had stepped through, after a quick glance into the street. Bates dropped a bar across the door, then turned to watch Slocum as he laid the girl gently on the one bunk in the cabin. When Slocum finally looked up he saw the unfriendly expression.

"One of 'em tried for me," he said shortly. "They got her instead."

Bates didn't say anything.

"I did what I could," Slocum said. "I was hoping you'd have a doctor friend in town. One with a close mouth."

Bates nodded. He glanced at the girl, then lifted the bar from the door and disappeared.

27

"I guess you had some rotten luck," Bates said. His tone was grudging, as though he hated to admit that he couldn't blame everything on Slocum.

"Yeah," said Slocum. "And I made some bad moves, too."

Bates rolled his shoulders in a shrug. "The man ain't been born yet that plays every card just right."

The two men spoke softly, barely making themselves heard over the crackle of the fire in the stove between them. The doctor had come and approved Slocum's stitches, pulling some of them and adding a few of his own after he shaved away a patch of Merry's hair. He didn't seem too worried about the girl. He put something on the wound and forced something else down her throat, and told the men she'd wake up when she was good and ready to face the world again. He had said he would look in on her from time to time.

Now Slocum glanced toward the girl's sleeping form on the bunk. "You're sure you can trust the doctor?" he said.

"He knows his stuff, if that's what you mean."

Slocum nodded.

"He'll also keep quiet," said Bates. "No one will know she's in town. Or you, for that matter."

Slocum nodded again. "Except I won't be here much longer."

"Got some unfinished business, I suppose."

So far Bates had not asked for any details, and even this last was only half a question, tossed off so that Slocum wouldn't feel he had to answer if he didn't want to. But Slocum was starting to feel a little better as he soaked up the warmth of the stove, massaging his stiff muscles. He began the story of the last three days, telling Bates about the chase from Deadwood, the meeting with Rousseau, alias Gerry Chambers, the escape from robber's roost, followed by Merry's meeting with the returning outlaw, and the shot that left her sagging in Slocum's arms.

"Musta been a bad moment," Bates said.

"I wasn't any too pleased."

The ticket seller nodded, and they lapsed into silence. The crackling and popping of the pine logs was a soothing sound.

"So you downed four of them," Bates said after a while. "Leaving four to go if you count Gerry Chambers. That ain't a bad day's work."

Slocum counted back. He'd killed Bill Chambers right after the fight. There was the man who fell against the cabin when they tried to make that first break for it. The man with the hurt leg. And Parker. Slocum smiled. "I guess I can only claim three," he said. "Don't forget the girl gave me a hand with one of them, and saved me a lot of trouble in the bargain."

"How could I forget?" Bates said. "She sure is one to ride the river with."

Slocum saw the man's gray eyes drift over toward the girl without trying to hide the feeling behind them. There was pride there, and tenderness, and a lot more. Slocum studied the sandy-haired man for a moment, then found himself looking around the little cabin with a different point of view. He saw the way the man had settled in here, just naturally, to make himself a home in a way that Slocum had never done. It only needed a woman to make it a real home.

Slocum now tried to imagine that this was his own cabin, that he would return here night after night, perhaps year after year, coming home from a regular job with a monthly paycheck. A peculiar feeling crawled along his skin, and he shuddered. It would make a difference, of course, if a girl like Merry Atwood was here to come home to. But in that moment he knew that his questions of the day had been answered.

It wouldn't make enough of a difference. Not for him.

"Slocum," said Bates.

The man's eyes seemed troubled. Slocum gave him his full attention.

"I have something to tell you," he said. "A confession, sort of."

"You mean about that thousand dollars of James East-man's?"

The ticket seller let his mouth fall open in surprise, glancing at the girl on the bed.

Slocum shook his head. "She never said a thing, Bates. Although that's what helped me figure it out."

The other man nodded, staring shamefacedly at the floor. "I should have known you were on the right track when you asked me about the ticket prices."

"Sure. Twenty-seven dollars to Cheyenne. Three hundred and five dollars in the wallet, which I found in Swearingen's safe. Leaving an even thousand dollars missing. The thing was, Swearingen acted like he was truly surprised when I asked him where the rest of the money was. And anyway, there was no reason for him to have taken out just that amount. I figured Merry had it hidden on her somewhere, but she didn't. Then there was the missing calling card to think about. And when she found out I didn't know, she only said she couldn't tell me."

"That was good of her," Bates said.

Slocum nodded. "But after that, of course, it wasn't too hard to figure out that she'd given you the money the morning she bought her ticket. After you told her how I came to have the wallet. She asked you to return it to the man's fiancée for her, didn't she?"

"Yeah." Bates looked at the girl again, his eyes warm at first and then turning sad. "I wonder what she must have thought of me," he said quietly.

"Maybe just that you were tempted. Maybe she figured you'd come around."

Bates nodded. "I had the draft made up this morning, in the name of that girl he was engaged to. I was gonna send it down on Thursday's stage."

Slocum reached inside his coat for the pigskin pocketbook and tossed it across into the other man's lap. "Might as well add the rest," he said. "You can refund the ticket, right? And send that along too?"

"Of course. And thanks." Bates went back to staring at the floor. "One thousand dollars," he whispered.

"Enough to make any man think twice," said Slocum. "I'm

not sure what I would have done myself. If I hadn't given my word."

Bates was quiet a long time, picking at his jeans with his big fingers. "I knew she wanted to escape," he finally said.

"You mean Merry?"

Bates nodded. "She asked me once, a while back. But I didn't have any money put away, and I couldn't afford to give up my job." The man's gray eyes came up to look at Slocum, then shied away. "I told her she could stay here, but she must have known what Swearingen would do." He passed a hand over his face. "I *hated* being so helpless. Especially when I . . . when I wanted her so bad. To lie here at night and think of what she was doing over there . . ."

Slocum grunted in sympathy.

"I don't know," Bates said, sounding defeated. "I tried a little prospecting whenever I had some time, but I can't tell a piece of ore from a damn piece of coal. I tried to save, of course. Then I tried cards." He was wringing his hands together. "And then a thousand dollars falls in my lap. It was like the Denver mint!"

"I know the feeling," said Slocum, squirming a little. "But now you have your chance."

The sandy-haired man looked up with a frown. "What chance?"

"You can take care of her. Protect her." Slocum leaned forward and lowered his voice. "You could probably marry her, of you wanted to."

"But her home . . ."

"Look at her, Bates. Do you think she could ever go back to Ohio? Do you think she'd ever *want* to?"

The ticket seller gazed at the still form on his bunk. "Even if she didn't, why would she have anything to do with me?"

"Damn it, Bates. Just how much do you want her?"

He nodded as if he understood what Slocum was saying.

"All right, then," Slocum continued. "You just take care of her and be good to her. She'll see what kind of man you are."

Bates stared at Slocum, a hooded look of mistrust. "What's your stake in all this?"

"I want her to be happy."

"That's all?"

Slocum nodded. "And I know I'm not the one who can do it."

"You saying I am?"

Slocum nodded again, looking around the little cabin. "You can give her the things she'll want, Bates."

"I ain't done such a great job so far."

"It's up to you," Slocum said shortly. "But I do believe you were the one that saved my ass the other night."

Bates looked down, with his heavy eyebrows bunching into a scowl. He tapped a boot on the hard dirt floor and finally looked up with a firm, resolute nod. "By God, Slocum, you're right. Listen to me whinin' like some wet-behind-the-ears kid. It's a wonder you didn't throw up."

Slocum laughed. "There's no accounting for the way a man will act when it comes to a woman."

Bates laughed too. "Ain't that a fact!"

The laughter gave way to smiles, but for Slocum there was a sudden heaviness in the throat. He listened to the fire for a few more minutes. Finally he sighed and went back to business. "Did you send my message?" he asked.

"Sure did, Slocum. The boss is on his way."

"How do you know?"

"Office sent a wire this morning. He'll be on tomorrow's stage."

"What time does it get in?"

Bates shrugged. "Somewhere around noon."

"That'll give them a twenty-four-hour head start."

"The road agents? They'd be long gone even now."

"There's still a chance, though. We could track them. Do you have any guards in town?"

Bates shook his head. "Brown will probably bring a couple with him, though."

"Sure. Sometime tomorrow."

"I know how you feel, Slocum. But hell, they're probably gone for good. I'd say you done your job."

"It's still unfinished business."

"You mean for what they done to Merry, right?"

Slocum nodded. He sounded as weary as he looked. "I guess

the only thing I can do is ride out again. Meet Brown some- where below Deep Springs. We could start tracking from there."

"What about Swearingen? He's the son of a bitch behind it."

"Yeah, but he'll still be here. He thinks he's safe behind all that protection."

Bates raised an eyebrow. "It is pretty good protection, Slo- cum."

"Yeah."

"But not from you?"

Slocum was thinking about Al Swearingen and his man Butcher, and he didn't realize what the thoughts were doing to his face. But Bates saw the way the lips pulled back over Slocum's sharp white teeth, and he saw a depth of cruelty in Slocum's eyes. Bates made himself a little smaller in his chair by the fire.

"No," Bates said softly. "I guess not from you."

28

Slocum was roused from two hours of sleep by the touch of Warren Bates's hand on his shoulder. He tried to wipe the grainy feeling from his eyes, but it was destined to stay with him for many days to come. Slocum sat up in the chair that had made him stiff while he slept. When he saw that Merry Atwood had not moved he glanced at Bates, who frowned and shook his head.

It was not long after midnight that Slocum eased himself out of the little cabin in Deadwood, leaving the light and the chair by the fire for a dark road and a cold saddle. He carried a gunnysack of hard biscuits, jerky, salt pork, and beans, pressed upon him by Bates. He threw the bag across his shoulder and let his eyes wander over the other cabins and into the shadows. There was nothing to tell him that he was being watched by hostile eyes, but suddenly he turned for a last look at Warren Bates closing the door behind him. He had a glimpse of the man's pale gray eyes, and the soft form of the girl beyond him, and then Slocum saw nothing more.

Slocum found his pony undisturbed behind the cabin and led the other horse down the gulch to the stage road. He covered the miles then as fast as he could, switching horses when one started to blow, and slipped by Deep Springs in the hour before dawn. He made his way carefully, out of sight of the station, on the chance that Gerry Chambers should still be there.

Slocum did not think it likely. He thought it more likely that Chambers had communicated with Al Swearingen the previous afternoon, discovering that Slocum and Lacey were one and the same man. Then, failing to find Slocum for the purpose of seeing to his permanent silence, Chambers would probably understand that his career in the Black Hills had come to an end. Slocum expected to find the stage station deserted. He expected that Gerry Chambers and his three remaining cohorts were already miles away across the plains. But being careful was a habit with Slocum, and he was getting too old to change his habits.

Slocum waited three miles below Deep Springs. The birds started to sing, and soon he could see the pines in the first gray light. When the stage came he stood in the middle of the road, hands high in the air, a friendly grin on his face. The driver thought he saw a trap and slapped the reins for more speed. But the guard clutching the short-barreled ten-gauge beside the driver was the one called Gene, and he said something in the driver's ear that brought the reins up short and the horses to a dead stop. The horses snorted and shook their big gray necks, prancing restlessly so the stage rolled back a few inches. The ugly snout of the Greener stayed rock-steady on Slocum, who grinned and didn't move a muscle except to say that he believed Mr. Brown was expecting him.

Horatio Brown poked his head through the window at the side and saw Slocum, then put both his hands to his mouth and called for the boys to come in. He had a few quiet words for the passengers to explain the delay, and a few more with the guard when that man demonstrated a reluctance to put away his weapon.

Two deputies hired by Harrison, Gilmer, and Salisbury led their horses from the forest. The guard jumped down from the box. They joined Brown and Slocum beside the road for a conference the passengers saw but could not hear. They heard nothing of the events described by the tall stranger with the green eyes, although they witnessed the excitement among the others. The more alert passengers may have seen the stage superintendent's eyes grew round when he learned that he had himself employed the leader of the gang. He compressed his lips in a determined expression. He returned to the coach, but the passengers were to remain frustrated. They were told only that they would have to make themselves as comfortable as possible beside the road while the stage went on without them.

• • •

Thus it was that an apparently empty coach pulled into the yard of an apparently empty stage station at Deep Springs. The driver called, but no answer came from the cabin. No smoke appeared from the chimney of stone and mud. The guard jumped down once again from his perch and carefully approached the door. He did so with the full understanding that the gang might have planned a final robbery to finance their escape, and that if this was a trap, he himself would be caught in a murderous cross-fire. But these were the daily risks accepted by the guards. In this case the risk proved to be nonexistent.

When the messenger discovered that the cabin and the corral were in fact empty, that the stove was cold and the nearby woods unoccupied, he sounded the all-clear. The two extra guards then raised themselves from the floor of the stage while Brown and Slocum cantered their horses in from the road. Brown dispatched the coach for the passengers before leading a thorough search of the surrounding country. There was no trace of the outlaws, not a fresh track to be found.

The stage returned and continued north without fresh horses for the last leg of its three-hundred-mile journey. The passengers went without breakfast. The driver was instructed to wire the company from Deadwood to begin the search for a replacement stationmaster. And the guard named Gene stayed with the coach for its continued protection.

Horatio Brown had untied his mustang from the rear of the coach to stay with the hunters. He and the extra deputies loaded their packs and bedrolls on the gelding that had once belonged to the outlaw Parker. Slocum had brought the horse with him only because it would have betrayed his midnight visit to Deadwood if Swearingen saw the outlaw's animal. But now he would be useful to lighten the burden on the other horses and speed the pursuit. Slocum handed out some of the jerky and biscuits from Warren Bates' gunnysack, and the four men drank their fill from Deep Springs before topping off their canteens and mounting up.

Slocum led them to the body of the man who had shot Merry, and then on to robbers' roost. Parker still lay sprawled on his belly on the ridge, and down below flies were crawling over the dead bandit leaning against the cabin. A fresh grave accounted for Bill Chambers.

"Brotherly love," said Horatio Brown.

"I hope Gerry will be able to tell us why they called him Persimmon Bill," said Slocum.

The hunters also found a valley empty of cattle and a broad trail leading southwest toward the barren stretches of Wyoming Territory. Brown said he was surprised they'd slow themselves down so much. Slocum said they probably needed money after the long winter, and pointed out that they'd have no way of knowing Brown and his deputies would be tipped off before they even got to Deadwood.

Slocum also told Brown, however, that it was possible the bandits knew Brown was coming. He startled the superintendent with his knowledge of the planned treasure coach, saying it came from the Chambers brothers by way of a passenger or employee on Saturday's stage. Brown compressed his lips even tighter and thanked Slocum, saying he had plenty to investigate.

The hunters burned the cabins in robbers' roost, and then pulled their Stetsons low over their eyes and headed into the sun.

A spring thunderstorm soaked them while they were still in the hills, and the sun parched their throats when they came out of the forest onto the wide sweep of sagebrush and cactus. By night the men huddled beneath blankets in cold camps, and by day the heat burned their cheeks and chapped their lips. Their dry skin cracked open, and alkali burned in the cracks. The winds blew at any hour, carrying sand that stung their eyes and made their throats raw. At times the trail they followed threatened to disappear, and it seemed that the hunters had endured their hardships for nothing. But in those times Slocum learned that the smaller of the two deputies, a half-blood Crow who had little to say, was a tracker of great skill. Slocum was thankful that he rode with this group of men, rather than in the group ahead of them. He would have been more sympathetic with the fugitives—which was where he normally seemed to cast his lot—except that he had never got around to liking them very much.

Not that he enjoyed his present company any better. If the tracker kept to himself, the other deputy acted like he was trying to make up for it by talking every chance he got. But it was the kind of talk that only shows a man's stupidity, and Slocum steered clear of the man as much as he could. Slocum liked Horatio Brown all right, but it seemed the superintendent had turned to brooding, as if he could think of nothing else until this job was done. Slocum resigned himself to keeping his own company. And reminding himself—as often as he could—of the two thousand dollars that waited for him at the end of the ride.

The grim-faced hunters followed the trail across flat-lands and over high plateaus and through wide basins of yellow grass. They crossed Beaver Creek on the second day out, and Lodgepole and Black Thunder. On the third day they struck the Cheyenne, following the trail along the creek bed even after the water had disappeared.

Here they climbed the side of a low butte and caught their first sight of the outlaws—a trail of dust perhaps ten miles off. Slocum saw a kind of light come into Horatio Brown's eyes. The superintendent said he figured the "varmints," as he called them, were hoping to sell their stock in the old Mormon river crossing up ahead on the North Platte. Brown worried that once they made Casper, the outlaws could split up and lose themselves among the population.

The hunters agreed to a short sleep that night, and by dawn they had already been in the saddle three hours. With first light the tracker was peering down at the trail along the dry fork of the Cheyenne. The other deputy was by his side, Slocum and Brown flanking them higher up on the banks of the wash. They had tied pieces of leather over the hooves of their horses to deaden the sound of the iron shoes. The four weary men scouted cautiously, working forward yard by yard, but there was little concealment in such open country. The hunters rounded a bend in the wash and saw their quarry in the same moment as the outlaws saw their pursuers.

There were shouts of surprise on both sides. Some men pulled revolvers, while others preferred their Henrys or Winchesters. Slocum saw Gerry Chambers break for his horse and

spur off into the sagebrush. Slocum was already running his
little pony to cut the man off. Chambers tried a couple of shots
over his shoulder, but Slocum hunkered low in the saddle, and
his spotted pony gained on Chambers in the first quarter mile.
Then Chambers concentrated on speed, and the long night's
ride began to take its toll. Slocum could hear the rattle in his
pony's lungs, and Chambers' fresh horse began to widen the
gap.

Slocum yanked on the reins and jumped from the saddle,
grabbing his Henry in the same motion. He kneeled in the sand
and brought the heavy rifle to his cheek. Chambers was wildly
spurring his horse, looking smaller and smaller by the second
over Slocum's sights. He took half a breath, held it, squeezed
the trigger, instantly levering the rifle to fire again. Then a
third time and a fourth. He was tracking Chambers for the fifth
shot when he saw the man's body sag and topple slowly sideways onto the hard-caked dirt.

Chambers was still alive when Slocum reached him. The
outlaw was trying to raise himself on one elbow and looking
for the gun he'd lost when he fell. Chambers gave up and
clutched at his side, where Slocum's tumbling bullet had exploded two ribs on its way out. The outlaw's body swayed with
his efforts to breathe.

"Not very sporting," he said, "to shoot a man in the back."

"I guess you deserve the same kind of treatment you give,"
said Slocum.

Chambers coughed blood into his black beard and tried to
spit at Slocum. "I should have killed you while I had the
chance," he said.

"Your mother probably felt the same way about you."

"Goddamned bastard." Chambers fell back, then tried to
raise himself again. He gave that up too. His eyes never left
Slocum, and Slocum was never sure just when Chambers had
died.

There was no more gunfire from the dry creek bed when
Slocum threw the body across the saddle of Chambers' horse
and began leading him back. He discovered that the outlaw
named Quince and the quiet little tracker were the only ones

who remained untouched by bullets. The talker had been shot low in the hip and was doing a lot of complaining, while Brown had been grazed just beneath the armpit. They were still better off than the other two outlaws, one of whom was gut-shot and not expected to live.

Guns were collected and precious water doled out while dust settled and the blue cloud of powder smoke drifted away in the wind. Slocum helped tear shirts for bandages and make the wounded comfortable. Brown would take them the few remaining miles into Casper for better doctoring, and a jail. Slocum and the deputies would herd the cattle and extra horses along behind, to be held for proper disposition.

No one could think about anything else besides a bed.

Four days later the small band rode into the dusty streets of Cheyenne, pulling the bodies of Gerry Chambers and the gut-shot outlaw in a spring wagon. The two survivors were jailed. Brown had sent wires from Casper, so the bloated bodies of Parker and the other two bandits—one of whom was never identified—were already being hauled in for a pauper's burial.

Slocum spent the better part of a day giving a deposition in the courthouse. That night, wearing a wide grin, he received a hefty packet of scrip from Horatio Brown, who was also smiling.

"Could this be the beginning of a new career?" asked Brown.

Slocum shook his head. "I'm too old to learn new tricks."

Slocum saw Brown again in the morning. The superintendent was no longer smiling. He passed over a telegram without comment. The piece of paper said: "UNABLE TO WORK STOP SERIOUSLY WOUNDED STOP SUGGEST REPLACEMENT STOP TELL SLOCUM MERRY ATWOOD MISSING."

29

Warren Bates looked up from his bunk and murmured, "You look right healthy, Slocum. I bet you're glad you was out trading potshots with desperate bandits."

Slocum smiled despite himself. "Uh-huh. There I was, making the road safe for the stage line while you were back here just taking it easy."

Bates tried to hold out his hand, but his face contorted with the pain of the movement. Instead he rested the hand across his chest, covering the blood-crusted bandages. After a moment he opened his eyes.

"The doctor claims he took out six slugs," said Slocum. "Was he talking about the whole bunch, or just you by yourself?"

"Has to be me," said Bates. "I sure as hell didn't hit any of the bastards." The ticket agent looked away, and his lips were trembling. "Damn it, Slocum, I feel pretty rotten for letting them take her like that."

"Six slugs can dampen your spirits some. How'd it happen?"

Bates frowned. "I still haven't figured out how they knew she was there—"

"Was she awake?"

"Yeah. Oh, that's right. She woke up the day after you left—that morning. Pretty sore, but she was coming along okay. That hole in her scalp was healing up real well."

Slocum nodded. "You had to leave her alone, of course . . ."

"Sure. She understood. She stayed in the cabin with the door locked. No one could have seen her."

"The doctor?"

"I trust him, Slocum. It had to be something else."

Slocum shrugged. "Someone might have seen me bring her in. Maybe they just took a good guess. It doesn't really matter anymore, does it?"

"I guess not. All I know is they came and got her while I was at work. Smashed my door all to hell and dragged her out."

"Anyone see it?"

Bates shook his head. "No one that'll talk, anyway."

"Did you see Marshal Sandler?"

"I like to observe the formalities."

"And?"

"He *uses* the formalities. I can't prove the girl ever existed, much less the fact that she was kidnapped. And we haven't even gotten around to who the suspects might be."

"You didn't expect anything different, did you?"

"Hell no! But it just made me madder."

"Ah."

Bates gave Slocum a rueful, hangdog look. "I guess I went off half-cocked," he said. "Went into the Gem with my guns out, throwing around accusations and demanding to see the girl."

"Wish I'd been there to see it," Slocum said with a grin.

"So do I."

"I take it you didn't have anyone to watch your back. Like I did."

A warm look passed between the two men, suspending the conversation for a moment, and then Bates was shaking his head. "That's where I was bein' stupid. They tried to kick me out, see, and somewhere in there a shot was fired. I don't think it was mine, but that doesn't matter either. There were more shots, and I got hit. I got to pullin' the trigger myself, by then, but my eyes were so full of blood I couldn't see a damn thing. Somewhere in there I collapsed, and they rolled me out onto the boardwalk. Butcher came out and said, 'Tell Slocum we want him.' That's the last thing I remember. I still don't know who got me to the doctor's."

"So that's the game," said Slocum.

"What?"

"I couldn't understand why they'd still be trying so hard to get the girl back. You just explained it to me."

"To get at you, you mean?"

"That's what Butcher said, isn't it? They must have been afraid I wouldn't come back."

"Wouldn't they be glad to be rid of you?"

Slocum shook his head. "I cost them too much, Bates. They lost their easy pickings along the stage road, plus most of the gang and a couple of the gunhands here in town. Thanks to me Swearingen killed one of his own customers. Even if he doesn't lose business he's lost more respect. And people probably don't fear him as much as they used to, now that they know he's not invulnerable. And Butcher—" Slocum grinned. "I guess Butcher and I just take a natural disliking to each other."

"Since you put it that way," said Bates, "I'm amazed you made it this far north."

"Let's hope our friends at the Gem will be just as surprised."

The ticket agent looked worried. "You going in alone?"

"Relax, Bates." Slocum let a smile grow across his face. "I brought along a little half-breed tracker and some big fellow who talks too much."

Bates tried to sit up before he remembered his condition. "Those two?" he said.

Slocum nodded. "Horatio Brown gave me a message for you. He said the company frowns on people who shoot up the help."

30

The two deputies trailed Slocum into the badlands toward the Gem Saloon, the half-breed pressing his lips together and looking intent. The other one was running off at the mouth about the time he stared down a grizzly in the Rockies, cheerfully telling his own story even though nobody was listening. Slocum was thankful that their job was almost done. He wasn't sure how much more of the talker he could stand. He wondered if the tracker and the talker always traveled together, and how the tracker endured it.

It was a Wednesday night at the end of May, and the dark streets seemed more full of life than ever. The fortune hunters who waited out the winter elsewhere were now swelling the spring trails to fight the rain and melting snow. The wagons that brought their supplies jammed the wide street, strings of mules and oxen patiently stamping in the mud. Slocum and the deputies pressed through the noisy crowds and set themselves apart by the purposeful way in which they walked. Here and there someone turned to watch the three dark shapes with hats tipped low over their faces, sensing a mission in their intent and deliberate progress. Some may have wondered about the shotgun slung over the arm of the short one, but no one recognized them.

Slocum halted in front of the Gem. The talker stopped in mid-sentence, the huge silver-tip grizzly of his memory or imagination still rearing over his head. Now he looked as grim as the tracker, and Slocum felt a little more confidence.

"This is the place," he said. "And don't forget that this is my play."

The big deputy nodded. The half-breed only stared.

"Mostly I need you to keep an eye on the customers," Slocum said. "Swearingen's fight is with me, and there's a chance—just a chance—his bunch will meet me head on. If they do, you stay out of it."

The talker nodded again.

"If someone wants to use my back for target practice"— Slocum grinned—"then you have my permission to interfere." He was serious again. "But let's not kill anyone we don't have to."

This time the tracker dipped his chin a quarter inch, and Slocum almost wondered if he'd imagined the movement. The half-breed was getting downright talkative. The big deputy sighed and shrugged his shoulders. "Might as well get this over with," he said.

They pushed through the door into the smoky light of the Gem, one after the other. Anyone watching would not have known who was with who. Slocum and the talker hesitated at the front of the room. The tracker, carrying his shotgun, walked immediately toward the door that led to the cribs—and Swearingen's back exit. Slocum didn't want anyone slipping out of the building to lie in wait outside.

A tough-looking brawler had watched the men come in from his place off in the corner, but Slocum figured him for a new man. The bartender—wearing a bandage on his shoulder and an ugly scowl on his face—was the first one to show recognition. He hollered something above the noise and then he ducked. Slocum began to draw, but the big deputy was already there, reaching down behind the bar. He moved much faster than Slocum expected.

The bouncer in the corner was beginning to figure out something was wrong. He shoved himself away from the wall, but Slocum had already started to yank his Colt on the bartender and now he kept it coming. The bouncer froze with his hands in the air. By now the deputy had hauled the bartender up by the hair with one hand and pinned his arm with the other. He worked his way down the arm and grabbed a revolver from the bartender's hand. Then the deputy folded the bartender in half, smashing his face down on the countertop. Slocum heard a crunch and saw blood begin to well out across the counter from the bartender's broken nose. The deputy looked like he was making himself comfortable, still holding the bartender's face to the counter. "So there I was without my rifle," the deputy said, "an' that damn griz just three feet away. Tall as a house, he was. Damned if I wasn't staring into the bastard's belly button!"

Slocum laughed. Anything for an audience, he thought.

The tracker had gone through the door to the cribs, and now Slocum saw another bouncer coming backwards through the door, arms raised high over his head. He glanced over his shoulder and saw Slocum. He was one of the toughs who'd gone on the search that first night, and now his arms jerked down as if he wanted to draw so badly he almost forgot about the odds against him. He glared at Slocum and let it go at that.

The saloon was beginning to go quiet as the customers noticed what was happening. They would stop and stare, some of them bored or annoyed—if they'd been in the West long enough—and some of them wide-eyed with excitement. Those were likely the ones who'd come west after reading dime novels, and now they were about to see some real excitement. Slocum felt a little disgusted, like some freak who'd put himself in a circus. He sidled over toward the piano player and yelled at him to stop the music, a little meaner than he had to be.

When he had everyone's attention Slocum told them the Gem was closing down and it was time to go. No one moved. The gold hunters and gamblers weren't used to being told what to do. They stared at Slocum, and he stared back. "All right, then," Slocum said. "Stay if you want. But the bullets are about to fly, and you better not be in the way. I'm sure you heard about the poor farmer who got himself killed here last week."

There was more silence, and Slocum was trying to guess who would be the first to go when he sensed a movement on his left. He spun on his heel and saw the dark curtain lifting over the entrance to Swearingen's office, just far enough to show a rifle. Slocum was already bringing his Colt around, and he let go two quick shots into the curtain above the barrel. The rifle froze an instant, and then the whole curtain ripped away as another of the toughs fell forward on his knees. His body curled around the rifle on the floor, twitching violently in a death tremor.

There was another explosion in the room, and Slocum looked around in time to see one of the other men go down—the one who'd backed in from the hallway. His eyes were still on Slocum, showing his hatred, but his body was crumpling with the impact of the deputy's bullet. The dying bouncer let the gun slide from his nerveless fingers, and the sound of it hitting the wood floor seemed loud in the room. The other tough still had his hands up, looking frightened as he shook his head slowly from side to side. Slocum nodded at him and then dipped his head once in thanks toward the deputy, who returned a cheerful grin and kept talking.

Someone in the crowd said, "I wonder what's happening at Number Ten tonight," and someone else laughed as the crowd began shuffling toward the front door. By now the ones who had looked bored to begin with showed a little excitement in their eyes. The ones who had started out being excited now looked sick and a little frightened.

The customers shuffled on out through the door and left the one living bouncer, the bartender, the piano player, and five of the dance-hall girls. Slocum saw the dark-haired girl among them, the one named Roberta. She was looking at him from beneath her eyebrows, and now she smiled. Slocum liked the smile, and what he remembered about Roberta. It was a thought to save for later. He motioned with his Colt toward the bar and suggested the girls, the piano player, and the bouncer take cover. All seven got up without a word and went to stand behind the bar.

Slocum moved toward the front door while he kept an eye on the entryway where the curtain had been. He closed the door and dropped a heavy bar in place across two brackets there for that purpose. He started breathing a bit easier. But it seemed strange to be inside a saloon and hearing only the sounds coming from outside. When he walked across the room the sound of his boots echoed off the walls.

Slocum pulled open the door to the cribs and told the tracker to come out. He pointed toward the entry where the curtain had been hung. "Just keep your eye on it," he said. "Anything moves, give it a warning first. Then let go."

The tracker nodded and settled himself.

Slocum went back into the hallway, to the first door, and kicked it in. The little room was empty. So was the next. In the third he found an old miner hitching up his pants and a frightened young girl crying on the bed. He told them to stay where they were. He passed Swearingen's escape exit and tried the knob. Nothing. He kicked in the next door and the one after that. Two more empty rooms. He kicked in the last door, and for an instant he thought he'd gone crazy.

The grubby soap seller was staring at Slocum over the barrel of a Winchester.

Slocum's natural sense of order almost killed him. Part of his mind wrestled with the question: What the hell is *he* doing *here?* The distraction was enough to cloud his instincts. The filthy con man was a little slow too, grinning at Slocum with the kind of face you might see inside insane asylums. His left hand was wrapped around the rifle, finger on the trigger, with the barrel propped across his upraised right arm—the one Slocum had smashed with his boot. The arm was wrapped in plaster-soaked cloth. It was heavy, and the rifle barrel slipped a little.

Especially when Slocum roared in a gut terror and anger that made the soap man flinch as he fired. Slocum was spinning off to the side as he yelled and bringing his Colt into play, the blast of the rifle rolling beneath Slocum's roar and fading right into the blast from the Colt. Slocum didn't feel anything hit. But he saw the little hole appear in the soap man's cheek, just below his right eye. The man's head snapped back, and there was a terrible stink in the room as he unloaded himself.

Slocum stared at the body as it fell, his arms suddenly trembling out of control and his lungs struggling for air. The soap man had had him spooked from the beginning, and now he'd come close to cashing Slocum's chips. Slocum heard the slap of footsteps in the saloon and rolled around the corner back into the hall, but it was Roberta running toward him across the room. She stopped when she saw him through the hall door, a look of terror in her eyes that disappeared when she closed them, letting her body sag in relief. Slocum was settling down.

When the girl opened her eyes again Slocum winked at her and put a finger to his lips. She nodded and went back toward the bar. Slocum fiddled with Swearingen's escape door.

"I've got a knife on her throat!" said Butcher's voice through the door.

Slocum frowned. "Okay, Butcher. What do you want?"

"It's your life for hers," Butcher yelled.

"How do I know you have her."

Butcher's voice sounded scornful. "You know."

Slocum shrugged. "Spell it out, then."

"The front door's open, Slocum. The gun better be on your hip or she drowns in her own blood."

Slocum walked slowly into the main room. He looked at the tracker and pointed him back toward the hallway. The other deputy still had control in front. Slocum stepped over the dead man in the entryway and hesitated before the door, wondering what kind of ambush might be set up. Since he'd expect one, and they knew it, he didn't bother with the usual precautions. He slipped the Colt easily into its holster and opened the door.

It swung in and revealed nothing in the office except a wide-open safe that was completely empty. Slocum frowned at that and noticed the disorder of the desk as he kept walking.

He circled through the little maze that led to the sitting room, where he found Merry Atwood curled up in the chair covered with yellow daisies. She wore a rough brown cotton dress that Bates might have found for her—and which might have given them away, he thought. Her hands and feet were tied, and a gag was stuffed in her mouth. She was desperately cringing away from the knife in Butcher's hand. He stood behind her, holding the knife beneath her delicate white chin with one hand and holding a gun in the other. He gave Slocum a look of satisfaction. "Glad to see you're playin' it smart," he said. After suffering at Slocum's hands so long, Butcher was enjoying himself. Slocum thought that was dumb.

"I'm here, anyhow, so let her go. Your fight's with me."

"*Is* it now? This bitch doesn't like the way I fuck her. Don't you think that's reason right there to carve her pretty little neck."

Slocum planted himself only a few feet away, turning his

body slightly off to one side. "I'd say that's reason to think of her as having some damn fine taste, asshole."

"Hey!" Butcher straightened a little but unfortunately didn't pull the knife away from Merry's neck. "Watch your mouth, Slocum, or I'll shoot you down right now."

"That's your plan anyway, ain't it?"

Butcher suddenly grinned. "Come to think of it, yeah." He looked mean again, glancing down at the girl. "But if you don't watch it I'll give you a little demonstration on why they call me Butcher."

"Nope."

"What's that supposed to mean?" Butcher growled.

"You do anything to her and you know I'll kill you. It's that simple."

The evil grin again. "You think you're that fast, huh?"

"I must be. You haven't got the balls to give me an even chance."

"You got that right, Slocum."

Butcher's mood turned ugly, and Slocum braced himself. His right arm was mostly out of Butcher's sight now. The outlaw didn't notice it's tiny movement.

"I don't give a damn about chances when it comes to you," Butcher said. "There's just one thing I want—and that's to see you dead."

Butcher started aiming his revolver, and there was a muffled scream from Merry. The big gun was raising slowly over her head, deliberately, as Butcher took steady aim. He'd seen Slocum's empty hands when he first came into the room, so when Slocum's arm came up he probably thought Slocum was only acting out of instinct, trying to ward off the final blow. But Slocum's arm swung up a little faster than Butcher's, and Slocum's hand seemed to explode. Twice.

Butcher's gun arm sagged, and he looked down at his chest. He saw his own blood there, beneath the flames where Slocum's Remington derringer had set the shirt on fire. Butcher looked at Slocum with an agony in his eyes that was terrible to see, even on Butcher's face. The outlaw looked down once more and saw that when he tried to take a breath the blood bubbled in those two big holes. Butcher put up a hand to feel them. His nerves lost their will, and his body folded down, starting to collapse over the back of Merry's chair. With a muffled shriek of terror she threw herself away from the chair and fell to the floor.

Slocum ran toward the front door and met the tracker in the office. The tracker retreated when he saw Slocum, who turned and quickly searched the rest of Swearingen's living quarters. A troubled frown was growing on his face. Only when he was sure the man wasn't hiding somewhere inside did Slocum bend down to pull the gag from Merry's mouth and untie her hands and feet.

"Thank God you came," she said as soon as she could. She repeated herself over and over while Slocum held her. "I never thought . . . I mean, there were so *many* of them. How did you do it? Thank God you came, Slocum. But how—" She glanced around, a troubled expression on her face. "Did . . . where's Mr. Bates? Is he with you?"

"No," said Slocum.

Merry's face fell.

"He tried a few days back," Slocum said. "Didn't they tell you? The fool tried to do it all alone."

Suddenly the girl was looking excited, joyful. "You mean those shots . . ."

Slocum was frowning. "Probably. He got hurt pretty bad."

"Oh no!" But the joy wasn't completely gone. Merry would seem distressed for a moment, and happy the next. "How bad?"

"He'll live. He just isn't up and around yet."

"He'll live? That's wonderful! And he came!" Merry was gripping Slocum's arm, and now she was crying like crazy. "He came!" she said. "He really came!"

Slocum could only look at the girl for a minute, baffled, thinking it was just some kind of hysterical reaction to all the fear and uncertainty. But as the girl kept crying and laughing and clutching Slocum's arm, he suddenly understood. He felt stupid for not understanding sooner.

Slocum smiled—a little wistfully, perhaps—and wondered when the wedding would be.

31

The wedding was in late June, when Warren Bates could get around fairly well with only the occasional help of his new bride. Slocum told him he was getting slower than ever, and Bates responded with a big slow smile.

Superintendent Horatio Brown came up from Cheyenne for the ceremony, and regretted accepting his ticket agent's resignation.

Slocum's wedding present was a small bundle. Bates accepted it with a quizzical look, as if he'd expected nothing at all. When he found one thousand dollars inside he looked stern and insisted on returning the package.

"No," he said. "Absolutely not."

"It's yours by rights," Slocum said. "If you hadn't interfered with that bartender, I'd never've been around to collect this."

"No," said Bates.

Slocum turned to the superintendent. "What do you think, Mr. Brown? It's the company's money, isn't it?"

Brown nodded, a twinkle in his eyes. "If I'd known about the incident in the Gem, I would have split the money right in the beginning. That's just what I'd'a done."

"No," said Bates, looking a little helpless.

Slocum winked at Merry and said, "Damn it! Can't a man give you a wedding present without going through hell?"

Bates shuffled his feet. "Aw, Slocum."

Slocum grabbed the ticket agent's hand and put the package back in his fingers. "That's enough," he said, glancing at Merry again. "Now you got two dreams that come true. Might as well enjoy 'em, because who knows if it'll ever happen again."

Bates shuffled his feet some more and thanked him. Merry

reached up and kissed him, but Slocum tried not to look at her again. It made him feel sort of hollow inside. He thought it was something about the way she was looking at him . . .

Late that night Slocum sat in the living quarters of the Gem Saloon with Roberta by his side, her head on his shoulder. They were sipping from crystal glasses of fine bonded whiskey.

The girl had staked a claim on the saloon the night of the big gun battle, as soon as it was obvious that Al Swearingen was gone for good. The general speculation was that kidnapping Merry was going too far, that Swearingen knew it, and that he'd decided to run away from a completely ruined reputation. He'd abandoned any right to the business, then, and in his absence Roberta decided no one had a better right to the place than she did. If anyone held a different point of view, they kept quiet about it when they learned that John Slocum was her partner.

Roberta had proposed the deal to him within a half hour after he killed Butcher, and Slocum had agreed. He figured it would be a hell of a lot of fun to back up a girl who could think that fast on her feet. And, of course, she had offered a few other inducements.

Now she snuggled a little closer and said, "What's wrong tonight, John?"

"I don't know. Maybe it's time to go."

Roberta studied him a moment but didn't say anything.

"I think you've got control of the place by now," said Slocum.

"Sure. Thanks to you I could hire my own people. And the town's accepted it, I think." She took a deep breath and let it out. "I'd love to know where Swearingen got to, though."

"You and me both! I don't think anyone will ever know why Chambers called himself Persimmon Bill." Roberta laughed, but Slocum's expression turned suddenly sour. "He's the one that pulled all the strings, damn it. He should have paid the highest price of all."

"Maybe he will," said Roberta. "Maybe it'll all catch up to him and he'll wind up a miserable old bum, getting run over in a railroad yard somewhere."

"Let's hope so."

A minute went by, and then Roberta put her hand on Slo-cum's chest, sighing with contentment. Her hand dropped slowly down, went between his legs, and Slocum squirmed.

"What's wrong?" Roberta said again.

Slocum shrugged.

"Is it Merry?"

"Why would—"

"Because she was special. For you. Don't you think I can tell when a man's in love?"

"Oh come on!"

"And also when he doesn't want to be?"

Slocum sipped his whiskey to hide a frown.

"She loves you, too," said Roberta. "You know that, don't you?"

Slocum didn't say anything.

"So I'm puzzled, Slocum. If you could have had her—if it makes you like this when you see her married to someone else—why didn't you go after her."

"Maybe I didn't really want her all that bad," he said after a minute. "Maybe I'd just rather ride my own trail."

"Maybe?"

"That's what it seems like, anyway."

"What if you're wrong?"

Slocum shrugged. "I don't know, Roberta." Suddenly he grinned and tapped his whiskey glass against hers, before he held it up between them. The cut glass sparkled in the light from the oil lamp.

"Here's a toast," said Slocum. "Here's to all the things we think we want. And the things we think we don't."

JAKE LOGAN